THE OTHERWISE

The Otherwise

Duff/Smith

suggestions/wip'.

Act. 2^3.33.

1.

PRINT ON SCREEN:

"It's TRUTH was Amazing.
O! Joy! SOLARIS-Like!
White and translucent
foams. It squirmed-un
fettered, energized in
Wondrous Coil!"

1746 Ian MacFisk. 'WITH THE JACOBITE ARMY IN LANCASHIRE'

THE OTHERWISE

An Original Feature Film

MARK E. SMITH & GRAHAM DUFF

ALSO BY GRAHAM DUFF

Foreground Music: A Life in 15 Gigs
The Future's Here To Stay: The Singles of The Fall

THE OTHERWISE
Mark E. Smith & Graham Duff

First published by Strange Attractor Press 2021

Cover illustration by Graham Humphreys
Design/Layout by Maïa Gaffney-Hyde

ISBN: 9781913689186

A CIP catalogue record for this book is available from the British Library.

Strange Attractor Press
BM SAP, London,
WC1N 3XX, UK
www.strangeattractor.co.uk

Distributed by The MIT Press, Cambridge, Massachusetts.
And London, England.
Printed and bound in Estonia by Tallinna Raamatutrükikoda.

CONTENTS

In memory of Mark E. Smith,
a hero who became a friend and collaborator.
It was an honour and a solid hoot.

MY TELEVISION IS ALWAYS ON...

Elena Poulou

Is there an active way of watching TV?

Yes.

Is there a way to relive what it was like to watch TV with Mark?

No.

Television can be an educational tool, a glimpse into the world of the others, a background noise, a ritual. Inspiring signals can come through the TV. The sounds and sights of series, both known and unknown, news programme intro music, jingles, TV ads from our childhood. Core sentences can evoke memories that are soothing. Or unsettling. Just like smells.

Mark said the first TV programme he remembered watching was *Watch With Mother*. It was sweet how he would sing "WEEEED! Bill and Ben..."

When we met, we realised we liked lots of the same shows and films: Orson Welles and Fassbinder, *Dallas*, as well as that other oil family: *The Beverly Hillbillies*. But Mark also showed me a lot of stuff I didn't know.

When I first visited him, we watched TV shows like *Bewitched* in the morning, and English comedy classics like *Rising Damp*, *Nearest And Dearest*, *Keeping Up Appearances* and *The New Statesman* with the great Rik Mayall, who we both loved. Later we went to the theatre to see Mayall perform the character when they were dumped by the TV channels.

We watched a lot of comedy: the Marx Brothers films and spoofs like *Fear Of A Black Hat* and John Waters and Mel Brooks films, especially *High Anxiety*. We enjoyed US comedy like *The Larry Sanders Show* with Rip Torn, and contemporary British shows like *Toast of London*. But we sometimes preferred children's programmes as they often were wittier than shows for adults, shows like *Chucklevision* or *Horrible Histories*. History was a big passion for Mark and *World At War* was a firm favourite. When Freeview came to life the Yesterday channel was on all day.

Mark loved Bette Davis films, like *All About Eve*, as well as James Cagney films, especially *White Heat*. He was a fan of *Double Indemnity*, and 'Ma' from *Public Enemy*, as well as French films, like the comedy *Heartbreaker*, or *Lemmings* with Charlotte Rampling, who we both liked.

When we first moved in together, we were too poor to own a TV so we would watch at his mother's house, or in the pub. Through watching TV with Mark, I learned a lot about British culture and society of the past and present. We would make fun of terrible daytime or morning programmes like *The Wright Stuff* and *Richard and Judy*.

He would make the everyday extraordinary, and amuse me by making even the most mundane daytime television show into a cartoon, a proto meme, a piece of art.

After Mark broke his leg in Great Yarmouth, Ed bought us a TV/VHS device and we could record Mark's typical cut up tapes again, as well as watch the ones he'd already made. He'd compile VHS's that were like a combination of a mix tape and a diary.

He showed me comedy like Lenny Bruce, Bernard Manning, Les Patterson, Bill Hicks, Rab C. Nesbitt – back in those days when you could still buy official VHS tapes. Mark's favourite films were *Zulu* and *Waterloo*. These videos would be watched a lot.

Sometimes we'd also tune in to crap TV like a Franz Ferdinand concert in Paris, as "school TV" as Mark would call it. Watching it in order to know what NOT to do, what NOT to sound like etc. Funnily enough, he also loved watching *Eurovision*.

Daytime TV, with its relentless jangly theme tunes, was very fruitful. Even the worst show on earth like, let's say, *Doctors*, was great entertainment when you watched it with Mark. Something that's very common on live daytime TV is mistakes. Mark loved those. The intro to the song 'Systematic Abuse' is a glitch from *This Morning*.

He enjoyed the randomness that comes with the TV programmes you don't control or choose. When you were watching TV with Mark he would often know what was about to come up next. This is something I'd experienced myself, but once I was with Mark it started happening all the time. We'd be watching TV and Mark would have just been talking about something, say an obscure American actor, we'd flick the channel and there they'd be. Or a show would come on TV and we'd suddenly see something that was connected with an idea we'd been working on or thinking about.

Often Mark would ask me to record TV sounds, either from beloved films, or satirical shows like *Alistair McGowan's Big Impression* and *Dead Ringers*. He'd always be creating something out of the everydayness of life. Be it an overheard conversation, a coincidence, or a snatch of film dialogue.

He liked the BBC ghost stories of M.R. James, as well as films like *Tales From The Crypt*, and of course *The Twilight Zone*. Mark was a story consumer and fan himself: he was in the Arthur Machen society and *The Prisoner* fan club. Although, he despaired at every film adaptation of Philip K. Dick's books. We went to see *A Scanner Darkly* in the cinema, but Mark was appalled – especially at Keanu Reeves's performance (Mark called him Kanoo).

We also watched mainstream series like *The Americans*, and I am very sad he didn't live to see the final season. We would watch German TV through a satellite dish, especially the soap opera *Gute Zeiten, Schlechte Zeiten* (*Good Times, Bad Times*). Mark even talked about The Fall covering the theme tune.

He would always find a way to make me laugh. He would do Carrie's stare from *Homeland*, I would do Brody's facial expression. Mark also could mimic that guy from *The OC* who ended up playing a cop in *Gotham*. We would dance to music programmes, he would sing the *Coronation Street* theme tune with the lyrics a lady walking around Prestwich in the 70s would do.

We would swap tapes and DVDs with our dear friends Charlie Ritchie and Rona Landragon. Charlie told me how he once took Mark to an old video store: a smaller version of Blockbusters. Charlie said there was usually nothing good to ever be found in there. But Mark was in there for 30 seconds and grabbed lots of great tapes like *Nearest And Dearest*. It was like he actually just knew it was there. Mark could find really good stuff without even looking.

Whilst away on tour, it's especially insightful to watch the local channels, the local news and ads, as well as the local soaps. We particularly loved the infomercials of the new country. I'd try and learn the language by watching say Spanish films with subtitles. Paradoxically, you also find unknown shows from countries other than the host country. So for example we saw an amazing Dutch series in a hotel in Athens, and a great French series in a hotel in Utrecht. The first time I saw *Brideshead Revisited* was in yet another hotel in Athens. Mark and I ended up watching it every day at 2 pm.

If I ever wanted to make Mark laugh, I would sing the theme tune to the best of my abilities. i.e. not quite accurately. Mark would also sing certain theme tunes and commercial jingles, especially Opal Fruits and a Caramac tune that he had invented, to the melody of 'Zabadak'. Another favourite was the Dallas theme tune, which changed every season. I actually played it on my Casio keyboard when The Fall had a show in *Dallas*.

Mark thought about television a lot. The song 'The Early Days of Channel Führer' is about Channel 4 being crap and not doing their job as a cultural channel. We even made songs about particularly hilarious characters from TV series, like Nate from *Gossip Girl*, and oblivious TV personalities like Matthew Wright. We would make cartoons about them, or write letters to newspapers about bad programming.

What would watching TV with Mark be like now, in the autumn of 2020? Right this minute, we would be watching our friend Mark Aerial Waller on Radio Caroline's isolation station *twitch tv*: making clay figures, playing Greek and Indian music (Mark and I had invented our own Bollywood dance routine). Mark Aerial Waller is an amazing person and artist, so warm and intelligent. He understood Mark's essence like no other. There is an unreleased film of his where Mark is playing Agamemnon.

Mark and I wrote a few scripts together. For example *The World Age 4*: a film script about animals taking over the earth. Countless little scripts and poems and letters remain, but these pieces of paper and my words cannot convey the magic that was Mark's spirit and his love of life.

Mark was so effervescent and creative, a true writer and inventor. In his always curious and unjaded state he would play with the most banal of storylines and embellish them. Observations of everyday life, thoughts and events filtered by his perception. He often took expressions from real life and made them feel like dialogue:

"See ya mate!"

"Yeah. See ya mate."

He overheard sentences and made them feel like poetry:

"Nobody has ever called me Sir in my entire life."

Fall songs are often script-like. When writing a script the aim is to form those images and ideas into words then turn those back into a visual medium, by performing and filming them. With Mark's songs he achieved that, too, by richly describing the scene, the images would unfold in the listener's mind.

Writing songs is ideally a description of the world around us, as well as the world inside us. One can also describe things that have not happened yet, and invent things. The unseen and unheard.

Graham Duff had been using tracks by The Fall in his hilarious show *Ideal*. Then one day he asked Mark to play Jesus. It was a stroke of genius. Mark and Graham stayed in touch and started working on some script ideas for a television series. A new type of *Twilight Zone* one could say.

The three of us became very good friends and later Graham invited me to play a pretentious choreographer called Astrid in a couple of episodes. Graham had a great team of actors and also acted brilliantly himself.

Thank you, Graham, for your friendship and for making this script with Mark. I believe Mark could have directed and written films, written books. But he chose the medium of song to express himself. Also because he thought that the music industry was lacking. So he wanted to create something new all the time. I still think of him as a writer. Not a songwriter.

Dear reader, I hope flashes of Mark's being come to your mind whilst reading *The Otherwise*. I feel sure Mark's voice and thoughts and writing and his spirit will permeate our lives and those of future generations. Like a drizzle, a gentle megaphone, like a notification on your phone – every day and night, reminding you of his presence and existence beyond his earthly being.

Elena Poulou – Autumn 2020

April 2014,
Cruelest 2
"Zip it, Oxbridge
Poet OAF!"

Dear Graham,

hope things evened out 4 you –
Will try hard for birthday could
do w/ sea a bit. Have been
deliriously ill couch bound last 4
weeks. Did attached for your perusal/
O. Lordi, Was in hallucegenic pox
"frenzy" at one point, so no idea
if good or not, still got 2-3
days. No worry 4 you if you're
had Chickpox can't they

find a funding cure 4 those things instead of kids w/ 3 dads 2 I was told at school in 72 Science will erase pain + desease by 2010 Well in constant pain 20hrs a day cos orthodox Dr. won't give codeines/pain killers to DRINKERS only Paracetomol, false drugs and Anti-depressants (mine: 4 Bed-wetters + deep depression (?!) I've never took anti depressants + don't

intend to pollute my
body balance of pure street
drug + water spirits
(as you can see, House-crazy),
Talking of spirits (alcoholic)
I'd like 2 bring 'em up later
in THE O.W. As you can
see made Clive Berry
older sister.
PREMISE being up to mid
18 century Wellwork had Wondrous
Spring Well Icelandic-like
but often produced –

things. The locals abused it
for sexual pleasure, the
drumming up of Angel babes
i for the infertile.
It's removed to punish-
ment by the Anti-Jurassic
Protestant Corp, loosely in service
of ethereal clan of Lady Anne
& Wonder White Witch.
Any way will continue
soon, got 2 get
mail. your pal
Mark

2

Scene: KITCHEN. DUSK

L + J sat

LEN: Bev's been telling Clare you're a good mate of that M.E. Smith fella.

JEFF: Nah, met him 2 or 3 times in Manchester.

LEN: So you lied to her.

JEFF: No, you know what it's like when you first meet a girl, trying to impress – we all do it!

LEN: (Stares) SO YOU KNOW HIM?

JEFF: Sorta why, have you got tapes or music to pass on?

LEW: (with scorn)
Tdapes? Music?

Jeff goes to fill kettle.

LEW: NO!

Jeff gets last beer out of fridge. looks at his nails.
Len stares at him.

LEW: CAN I ask you something serious, Jeff?

JEFF: (trying 2 break ice)
Sure, Po-tential Bro'-in law!

LEN: Did he send you here?

JEFF: What? Oo?

LEN: You EARD. SMITH

JEFF: Mark? No!

LEN: I Bet, Is he PREZZY?

5.

JEFF: (sneering) Does that mean
cracked round 'ere like.
LEN: (shouts) NO! Answer
Jeff: (nervous) PRESTON?
LEN: PRES-BY-TERIAN.
Jeff: Not as far as I
know.
(Len Grunts, leaves kitchen.
JEFF: gets cup + bottle goes
toward kitchen sink whispers to
self: What a Wanger!

6

Muusic ----Presby

BAM THUD

A large grey/white object hits kitchen window w/MAX. force but not breaking it. floor shakes

JEFF grips steel sink, white _OWWOWW NOR AGAIN (childl.)

n Minks: heartbreaking in a man

12 Second Flash Back

W/CR.

JEFF: (Manly) GETHE HIM

7

fast,

Greyness (slide?)

Jeff: off we go. alright.

out.

(gets medium knife ~~out~~ ~~inside ride hand upward~~ out right hand inwards + upwards. Bottle in drinking pos. left. hand)

Opens back door steps down.

Surveys back garden

takes breath

(8)

2:
Stairs,
Hears sudden, erratic steps,
Skips at side of
cottage twirls round
corner. Crouched
JEFF: HOW'S YOUR DICK
TONITE?
IT'S CLARE, SMILING SHE LOOKS
AT HIM SIDEWAYS
CLARE: hiya Jeff, what's up!
JEFF: I was in the kitchen
then something. I was doing
...

(9)

I'm doing
this too much lately — Do
you ? Start thinking about
something... er .. then.
youre

CLARE: Sounds great! Give us
a shout next time! Ben's
gone straight ups so I
thought .. I'd grab a
solitary smoke.
For a change.
Want some?

JEFF: takes joint sez 'Well

CLARE:

ERR - Well then, (long laugh,
See ya!
(Doesn't move)

Jeff's poleaxed this is not studio Clare of grim smile bun-hair + jeans
Her full smile reveals small yellow pointy teeth her hair's all over the place Vic-torian dress to the neck
Suddenly a strong sexual ~~tingle~~ rises up thru his body. He goes in

kitchen. Clare skips off
into night. Jeff is
erotic daze he's not
felt like--- (11)

Jeff: THIS IN 2 and half
years. before the flat.
(takes 2 steps, stops)

SLAPS Right side of
face very hard, twice

JEFF: Grow Up.

To be Cont'd.

FRENZ

Friday February 16th 2007

I'm waiting in the reception at the BBC Building on Oxford Road in Manchester. I'm waiting to meet Mark E. Smith. I'm nervous. I wish I wasn't. But I am.

I've met quite a few famous people during my career: actors, singers, musicians, composers, writers, directors and so on. Over time I've managed to train myself not to get nervous or overawed. I've learnt to be myself and relax. Despite suffering from an acute case of imposter syndrome, this almost always works: but not today. Today I am definitely nervous.

This isn't even our first meeting. I've actually met Mark multiple times over the last 30 years. Although to be fair, these have predominantly been fleeting moments after Fall gigs, where our exchanges have largely been of the 'That was amazing' and 'Cheers cock' variety.

I first became fascinated by The Fall in the summer of 1978. I was fourteen, and a very recent convert to punk music, when my school friend Steve Dunn lent me his copy of *Short Circuit Live at the Electric Circus*. A various artists album, this was The Fall's vinyl debut. On the strength of just two snub-nosed songs featured on this release, The Fall immediately became my favourite group.

Within weeks I'd bought their studio debut: an EP entitled *Bingo-Master's Break-Out!* I was deeply impressed by how each song suggested its own secret world. In fact, I was so inspired by Mark's words I copied them out in the back of a school exercise book in blue biro so I could read them in isolation.

Two months later, I saw The Fall play live, in a place called Kelly's, on Amber Street in Manchester. The group's attack, their intensity and their otherness connected with me directly. It was more than just music. It felt like another realm was opening up.

By then, I'd already attended a few gigs: The Jam, The Clash, Suicide, The Rezillos, Gang of Four and 999. Each one of those had been genuinely thrilling experiences. Yet, by the end of The Fall's set, performed in a venue so small there wasn't even a stage, I realised I had just seen the best gig of my life.

Before I left Kelly's, I had to let The Fall know how good they were. The audience was clapping and cheering, Mark was standing by the amps, wearing a drab green shirt and talking to drummer Karl Burns. I tapped him on the arm. He turned around, looking slightly bemused as I gave him a thumbs up.

"That was amazing," I said, raising my voice above the applause.

"Cheers cock," he said with a confident little nod before turning back to Burns.

As I walked out of the venue that night, I couldn't have known that decades of Fall albums and singles lay ahead of me. Or, that I would go on to attend another 49 Fall gigs. Some of which would be even more exciting than that first one: although none would be quite as inspirational.

At fourteen, I had already decided I wanted to be a writer. So, under the influence of *Hancock's Half Hour* writers Ray Galton and Alan Simpson, *Doctor Who* writer Terrance Dicks, and Mark E. Smith himself, I began to fill endless notebooks with stories and scripts and ideas.

▲ ▲ ▲

Three decades later and I'm still filling notebooks. I'm now in the fortunate position that some of these ideas are being made into TV and radio shows.

I'm currently finishing off writing the scripts for the third series of my TV sit-com *Ideal*. It revolves around a lazy Salford-based weed dealer called Moz, played by Johnny Vegas. Unsurprisingly, I've already used quite a bit of The Fall's music on the show's soundtrack.

In the upcoming series, there's a storyline concerning a mentally disturbed Christian builder called Alan. Alan has a vision of Jesus who instructs him to kill Moz. But I don't imagine Jesus with a beard and flowing robes. I want him to look like some guy you might meet down the pub. Suddenly it becomes obvious who has to play the role of Jesus.

The show's production assistant finds Mark's contact details, and I send him a letter asking if he might fancy coming along to play a Salford messiah. To my delight, it turns out Mark and his wife and Fall keyboardist Elena Poulou are already fans of the show.

The letter he sends back to the production office is signed

All the best,
Your Lord
M.E. Smith.

▲ ▲ ▲

I'm not sure whether it's a good omen or not, but when the clapper board is lifted into shot for the first take of Mark's scene playing Jesus, miraculously it turns out to be slate number 666. This elicits a wave of uncertain laughter through the crew. Mark is clearly out of his comfort zone and initially struggles with running though the material. He's a man who famously doesn't like to do exactly the same thing twice. So repeating the same lines over and over is something of a struggle. Peter Slater, the actor playing Alan, has his work cut out to keep the scene moving, as Mark's delivery becomes increasingly fragmentary.

In the end, director Ben Gregor manages to tease out a subtle and funny performance. The final on screen result – Mark bathed in a golden glow, giving foul mouthed godly instructions, soundtracked by the strange celestial sounds of Coil, is the highlight of the third series. And it's definitely my proudest TV achievement.

Following the recording, I sit talking with Mark in his dressing room. I ask if he's ever thought about writing narratives for TV. He says a few years ago he'd developed some horror ideas for a Welsh TV company.

"Nothing came of it in the end. I think they lost them or summat." I say if he's interested in resurrecting them I'd be keen to help him pitch them to TV companies.

"Definitely," he says. "I'd like to do something that's really weird and properly frightening."

There's a knock on the door and Johnny sticks his head into the room. He clocks the two of us sitting next to each other and laughs, "look at the pair of you!"

It's time to go and do a photo shoot. First of all Mark, Johnny and Peter are photographed in the loft set. Then Mark, Johnny and I are photographed sitting on the couch in the living room set. The whole time the pair of them are cracking gags and making the entire room laugh. The moment feels so unreal I can scarcely take it in. Johnny turns to me, narrows his eyes.

"I get the feeling you've engineered a whole three series of this just so you could get in the same room as him." It sounds so plausible that I have to quickly scan my motivation circuits.

After the shoot, it's lunchtime. I ask Mark if he wants to come and eat on the catering bus. He declines, saying he'll go outside and have a smoke instead. We swap numbers and say goodbye. I watch him wander out towards the reception. 'Imagine how insane that would be,' I chuckle to myself. 'If we actually ended up writing something together!'

▲ ▲ ▲

It's three weeks later. I'm doing some washing up in the kitchen, when my wife Sarah comes through from the living room. In a comically casual voice she says, "Mark Smith's on the phone for you." She knows how unexpected and exciting an event this is for me. I dry my hands, walk into the living room and pick up the phone.

"Hi Mark. You okay?"

"Yeah not so bad pal. I wondered if you wanted to meet up and talk about writing some supernatural stuff together for TV?"

Yes, this is *exactly* what I want to do.

We make a date for me to go up to Manchester so we can spend an afternoon talking through ideas.

"I've just got a new office in town to do writing and shit," he says. "We could meet there."

"Yeah, cool. That sounds like a good idea." I try to give the impression I'm unruffled. I ask him for the address, but he says he doesn't have it to hand and will call with it nearer the time. As I put down the phone, my mind is whirring: 'Good God... We're actually going to do this.'

A couple of days before we're due to meet up, Mark telephones again. He says he's decided not to rent the office after all. Maybe we should meet somewhere else? I tell him I'll book a room at the BBC building on Oxford Road.

So now, here I am: sitting and waiting, and feeling nervous. Because even though we've already met officially, chatted on the telephone and agreed to work together, he is Mark E. Smith and I have been feasting on his thoughts for 30 years.

He walks into the BBC reception on time. He looks smart and relaxed, dressed as always in back trousers, polished leather shoes, a white shirt and suit cut leather jacket. Whether on stage or in the street, his image is unchanging. We say hello, shake hands and my nerves drain away.

A young man shows us to a small meeting room, with floor to ceiling blinds covering the glass wall. I've written a few notes in advance, but I didn't want to start working on anything in earnest, until we've had a proper talk about the kind of project it might be. All we've decided up to this point is that we'd like to write a horror/supernatural anthology series. And that it should be, as Mark has pointed out, "really weird and properly frightening."

Initially, rather than talk about our own ideas, we discuss our shared admiration of Rod Serling's seminal US TV anthology series *The Twilight Zone* and *Night Gallery*. As serious Fall scholars are aware, these shows were a formative influence on the young Mark, and, over the years, he's taken a number of *The Twilight Zone* episode titles and deployed them as song titles: 'Time Enough At Last' is inspired by the 1959 episode of the same name. 'Paranoia Man in Cheap Sh*t Room' is extrapolated from the 1960 episode 'Nervous Man in a Four Dollar Room', 'Nate Will Not Return' is corrupted from the 1960 episode 'King Nine Will Not Return', whilst 'Kick The Can' is taken from the 1962 episode of the same name.

My personal favourite *Twilight Zone* episode has always been 'The Masks'. Written by Serling, it concerns a family who don grotesque Mardi Gras masks which transform the wearer's features so they resemble the masks. Mark remembers this one too, but his favourite is the segment from *Night Gallery* entitled 'The Escape Route'. Also written by Serling, it concerns a Nazi war criminal who is haunted by his past and, having been recognised by a concentration camp survivor, ends up trapped inside a painting depicting his own crucifixion. Both stories have an atmosphere of dread and their own perverse internal logic. We agree that these are the kind of tales we should be writing.

I mention a thought I've had about basing all our different stories in the North West. Not just Manchester or Salford, but the surrounding towns and villages with old, twisted names like Sabden and Hall-i'-th'-Wood. Or Todmorden: a location with the reputation of being the UFO hotspot of Europe.

I'm especially keen to set something around Pendle Hill. Between the ages of 6 and 18, I lived in the town of Great Harwood. When I walked out to the playing fields behind our house, I could see the huge hump of Pendle looming over the town. With its history of ancient witchcraft and its damp, green grass, thick with magic mushrooms, it had always seemed to be a site of supernatural potential.

Mark has long been fascinated by magick and witchcraft. Throughout the decades he's made multiple references to these subjects in his lyrics. 1986 saw The Fall release the song 'Lucifer Over Lancashire' – although Mark had been working on versions of the song's lyrics since at least 1977. The final text is ripe with references to *'a demon's grip'*, *'his cock-eyed moon'* and *'A useless priest'*. It also contains one of the most viscid of Mark's lines: *'Monstrous kiss, wet dagger'*. I'd love to think we could get some of this ghastly atmosphere into a script.

I ask if he has any potential stories in mind.

"Sorry Graham, I've not done me prep," he then clears his throat. "I did have an idea for one called 'The Death of Standards'."

I'm thrilled by the fact he already has a title for it. And what a title! He goes on to outline the bare bones of a story about a woman who works in local government. On her drive to work she perpetrates a hit and run. Upon arriving at the office, she rants to her staff about how hit and run drivers should be executed. Then members of her staff start behaving in the same odd manner: performing terrible acts then raging against those very acts. This sounds exactly like something I'd love to watch.

We've been working for about 45 minutes when Mark lights a cigarette. The BBC building is, like pretty much every other building in the country, a non-smoking building. Mark knows this. I know this.

"You're not allowed to smoke in here," I say dutifully. Mark nods and purses his lips.

"They'll let us know if they have to."

We talk for a few more minutes, then the door opens a crack and a young, dark haired woman sticks her head into the room.

"Erm, you're not allowed to smoke in here," she says in a slightly apologetic voice. Mark looks up and gives her a charming smile.

"Oh? Sorry love – didn't know." He stubs out his cigarette on the sole of his shoe. She smiles back and closes the door. Mark turns toward me.

"Let's do another hour, then go for a drink."

An hour later, we duly move to *The Space Bar* further down the road. We sip from bottles of pilsner, as we continue to chew over story ideas. I mention the scenario from the 1979 Fall song 'A Figure Walks', wherein a character endures a long walk home during which they have their anorak hood zipped right up, restricting their vision by two thirds, as they are followed by a strange, alien monster.

"Could we use that idea?"

"Maybe," says Mark with a doubtful expression. I shake my head.

"Sorry, forget that. I know you're not really interested in going back to old ideas."

"No, not really. What's the point? I've already fuckin' done it. It's like I get these idiots ringing us up, asking the group to come and play *Hex Enduction Hour*. They wanna fuckin' grow up! You see, the further North you go, the less interested in the past people are. You get me?" I nod. But I'm not sure if I do get him.

"*And* the less interested they are in fuckin' 'celebrities'. You get too much of that in London. That's why I'd rather stay here, see what I'm saying? People here, they give you some fuckin' space. It's like this cunt here. I saw him clocking me when we came in."

Mark nods towards the table opposite. The occupant appears to be a casually dressed, well-to-do middle-aged Middle Eastern businessman, on a night out with his much younger girlfriend. That this guy might have recognised Mark, or have even *heard* of The Fall, seems fairly unlikely. Luckily, neither he nor his girlfriend seems to have heard Mark's assessment.

We stay in *The Space Bar* drinking and chatting for another three hours. Thankfully, at no point in proceedings does the middle-aged Middle Eastern businessman come over and ask for Mark's autograph.

By mid evening Mark is lively, engaging and drunk, whereas I am just drunk. Alcohol isn't really my drug. I can go for a month or so at a time without drinking and not really notice. Neither of my parents are drinkers either. Not for moral reasons: it's just never been part of their or my lifestyle.

For Mark however, alcohol has been one of his constant fuels. But if truth be told, pilsner and whisky are not his only vices. In fact, earlier in the afternoon, he had referred to having recently taken some acid whilst away on tour. I imagine relatively few 50-year-old men still take acid. And I would venture fewer still regularly indulge in biker's speed.

We push open the heavy glass doors of the bar. We step out onto the cobbled street. The sudden fresh night air almost *stings*. Mark still has a whisky tumbler in his hand. He takes a couple more gulps then drops the heavy glass into a refuse bin. He hails a taxi. I tell him I'll write up some notes on the stories. We say good night. We hug.

"Take it easy cock." Mark smiles as he climbs into the back of the taxi. I've had such a funny, inspiring and creative day. I'm fizzing with positivity. As Mark drives off I almost wave.

I hear my brain saying 'You're developing a supernatural anthology series with Mark E. Smith.' It seems highly unlikely. Almost like something that might happen in a dream, or in a supernatural anthology series.

As luck would have it, I am staying at the Palace Hotel, which is conveniently located directly across from where I'm standing. I'm about to stride blithely across the wide road. I suddenly stop, and remind myself that I am very, *very* pissed and that I should be extra careful. I take a deep breath then make sure I note the location and speed of all the cars and buses so that I can cross safely.

I step confidently out in front of a cyclist. He swerves to avoid crashing into me.

"Sorry!" I shout after him.

"Pisshead!" He shouts back.

▲ ▲ ▲

Monday April 30th 2007

I've caught the train from Brighton to London, in order to meet Mark. Following our previous meeting I wrote up our best ideas into three pages of notes and thoughts and posted them to him. He phoned me and said he loved them, and that we should meet again and carry on developing the material.

He and Elena are in London for a couple of days, whilst he does interviews and publicity work for the release of the album *Tromatic Reflexxions* by Von Sudenfed: a trio consisting of Andi Toma and Jan St. Werner aka German electronica artists Mouse on Mars, with Mark providing vocals and treatments.

On the train up to Victoria I was listening on my iPod to the Von Sudenfed track 'Family Feud' which has been released as a taster in advance of the LP. It's a lattice of rhythmic electronics and serrated beats, over which Mark declaims *'I am the great M.E.S.!'* We're so used to rap artists boasting of their skills and magnitude, but it's a rare thing for a left field rock artist to do it. Yet it's been one of the weapons in Mark's lyrical armoury from the very start.

I arrive at the Hilton hotel on Holland Park Avenue and take the lift up to his room. I knock on the door and a moment later Mark opens up, giving me a broad smile and a hug.

"Come in pal, come in. I've missed you."

This strikes me as an extremely sweet thing for him to say, considering we've only really met properly twice before.

We sit down at a small circular table by the window. Mark shows me the latest edition of *Wire* magazine, with he, Andi and Jan on the cover. He then produces two bottles of pilsner. We open them and talk about what we've been up to, after which Mark clears his throat and speaks in a serious voice.

"So, what's this meeting about then?"

For a second I feel caught out. Then I remember it was his idea to have the meeting in the first place. We read through the notes and soon we're both sparking off new thoughts about the series.

Elena enters wearing a dark blue coat and carrying a shopping bag. This is the first time she and I have met, but she's warm, friendly and clearly very smart. Elena and Mark have been married for six years and the love between them is palpable. When they first met, Mark was at his lowest ebb, with no group, and as far as the outside world seemed to be concerned, no great prospects for the future. But with the support and care of the Grecian Elena, Mark has risen again to a new level of artistic engagement and media presence.

"Can I get anything for anybody? Something to eat? Beers?"

We open a couple more pilsners as they talk about where they might eat later. Elena asks if I'd like to come along, but I have to decline, as I need to get back for a friend's birthday drinks. Somehow the conversation gets onto diet and I mention that although I don't eat meat I do eat fish, as I don't have any emotional response to fishes.

"The thing about you Graham," says Mark, "is you're nice." I wait for him to elaborate. He obviously isn't going to.

"So is that a good thing or a bad thing?" Mark lets out a full-throated cackle, takes a sip of his pilsner and clears his throat.

"Next subject!"

Elena leaves us to carry on working. We spend another couple of hours elaborating on some of our ideas. Mark also comes up with a new one. This story concerns one of those big Victorian factory buildings in Manchester that are inexorably being converted into flats. The building in question is haunted by the poor-house children who used to toil there in the late 1800s.

Mark suggests we call the series *The Inexplicable*. I love it, as it sounds like the title of an album by The Fall that I should already own.

▲ ▲ ▲

Over the following weeks I start working up the pitch document. Mark posts me an A4 envelope with more ideas and notes. It also contains a loose disc. It's a *Twilight Zone* DVD. Mark's spidery writing informs me that the disc 'fell out of the wall.' As fate would have it, the DVD features my favourite episode: 'The Masks'. I decide this is a good omen. Mark and I put together what we think is a strong pitch for the anthology series. I send it to a series of production companies. Unfortunately, nobody seems willing to take a risk on the idea.

▲ ▲ ▲

Nine months later, we decide to retool the pitch, so that the supernatural events all revolve around one character – a hapless electrician. Mark has the idea of developing it into a musical where the characters lip-synch to songs. Like *The Singing Detective*, but with all Fall songs. I immediately realise this is exactly the project that western culture has been lacking: a supernatural Fall musical for TV. It's so obvious when you think about it.

Once again, I find myself in meetings with commissioners who don't quite get it. I try and explain how many people believe Mark is a deeply significant artist. How he exerts a fascination even for those with no interest in The Fall. I say people would love to see what he might create for narrative television, and critics would be falling over themselves to write about it.

"Yes," replies one commissioner with a thin smile. "But he's not exactly Stephen Fry, is he?"

"Perhaps he's a working class Yang to Stephen Fry's posh Yin. Maybe they should star as a detective duo: Yin and Yang." He wrinkles his nose and replies in all seriousness:

"I doubt Stephen would be interested."

I begin to wonder if the title *The Inexplicable* is a hostage to fortune. I visualise a sarcastic review in the *Daily Mail* that concludes with '*…the one truly inexplicable thing about this show is why it was made in the first place.*' Then I fantasise about putting that review on the DVD cover, in an act of creative spite. After a few more unsatisfactory meetings with producers, *The Inexplicable* goes back on the shelf.

In 2011, Mark phones up and asks if I'd like to do a couple of gigs supporting The Fall, presenting some kind of performance piece. My immediate thoughts are 'God yes!' and 'Oh fuck!' After I put down the phone I ponder for about 5 minutes then I call up my good friend Malcolm Boyle. He's not only one of my very closest friends, and a long time creative collaborator, he's also the biggest Fall fan I know. If there's one person who needs to support The Fall, it's Malcolm. I ask if he'd like to do the shows with me.

"God yes!" He says, before adding "Oh fuck!"

In the end, I come up with the idea of doing an interactive quiz with audience members. We write the questions together and Malcolm and I appear as our characters from *Ideal*. He the pretentious art gallery owner Warren Keys, I the bitchy promiscuous and defiantly queer Brian. The quiz is called *How Northern Are You?* It involves asking audience members multiple choice questions:

In June 1976 a concert at the Free Trade Hall in Manchester changed the northern face of the north forever. Who was the concert by?

a) Emerson Lake and Palmer.
b) The Sex Pistols.
c) Freddie 'Parrot Face' Davies.

And…

The North's best artist Mr Lowry is famous for painting what?

> *a) Matchstalk men and matchstalk cats and dogs.*
> *b) Hatchlings stalking marching men in bogs.*
> *c) Matt Goss talking in matching hat and coat.*

The first gig is at Manchester's Royal Exchange Theatre. I used to come here as a schoolboy on trips with our drama teacher Mrs Grimshaw. It was the first place I ever saw live theatre. When I was 15, I witnessed a production of T.S. Eliot's *The Family Reunion* here, starring Avril Elgar and Edward Fox, complete with white noise scoring and towering eight-foot high ghosts in bright white gowns. It blew me away and remains the most frightening theatrical experience I've ever had.

Although going on stage to support The Fall probably runs it a close second. Rock music and stand-up/spoken word are an uneasy alliance at best. A rock audience expects to be able to talk throughout the show, and that can make for a tough gig. Another factor at play at the Royal Exchange is that this is theatre in the round. When you're performing, the audience is all around you. Henry Normal, the performance poet, renaissance man and top notch bloke, once remarked that performing in the round always makes him paranoid – because he can hear people laughing behind his back.

It's a weird experience sure enough. When Malcolm and I start our set, the theatre is only a third full. It fills up gradually, but it's hard to engage an audience when the majority of them are finding their seats. In the end we more or less pull it off. We get some game audience members up and the questions provoke a mixture of stares and laughter. It's a very incongruous event, but most importantly of all, Malcolm and I can now say we have supported The Fall. The 14-year-old me ascends to some higher chamber of bliss.

Our second support gig is at The Laugh Inn in Chester on November 28th. This is the group's last show of the year and the set includes The Fall's interpretation of the 1948 country and western song 'Blue Christmas', made famous by Elvis Presley. It seems an unlikely inclusion amongst the group's abrasive garage rock. Yet there is nothing ironic about the performance, with Mark delivering the lyric with mournful sincerity.

The following year, The Fall release a limited edition 7" single for Record Store Day. It comprises 'Victrola Time' and a live version of 'Taking Off'. The sleeve features an image of Mark and Elena taken at the Manchester Royal Exchange gig. The release has been given the title *Night of the Humerons*. I ask Mark if the title is a nod to Malcolm and my contribution to the evening. Mark chuckles.

"What do you think?"

I am flattered beyond measure.

In late 2013, Mark and I decide to take another look at the material we amassed for *The Inexplicable*, and explore the possibility of combining elements from a couple of the stories into a film script. Over the next year, there are more meetings in pubs, bars and hotel rooms. Mark sends me more brown A4 envelopes through the post. The contents are a mixture of scenes of dialogue written in Mark's distinctive yet indistinct scrawl, along with notes for future scenes. I mention my reservations about the title. Mark agrees and we settle on *The Otherwise*. I'm pleased to note this still sounds like the title of a Fall LP I should already own.

A few weeks later, I spend five days working away in Bath, directing rehearsals for the forthcoming Count Arthur Strong live tour. Rehearsals tend to wrap around 5pm, so in the evenings I give myself a project. I'm going to finish off the script for *The Otherwise*.

As I arrange the material on my hotel bed, it hits me that over half of it is already done. We've mapped out the whole narrative. I have several scenes on my laptop that we've written together, plus a pile of handwritten scenes from Mark, my notebook and recordings of our brainstorming sessions. I spend five evenings typing away, as I listen to The Fall's most recent LP *Re-Mit*. By the end of the week, the first draft is complete.

When I get home I print it out and post it to Mark, accompanied by a letter, the main gist of which is 'everything is still up for grabs.'

I don't hear anything back from him for nearly two weeks. I suspect he hates it. Then one afternoon he calls me up. He's in good spirits, chatty and convivial. He asks after my 25-year-old son

Misha – whom he knows from accompanying me backstage at Fall gigs. Mark has always been welcoming and inclusive and after the last Fall gig he gifted Misha a bottle of whisky as we left.

Mark asks me what I've been up to. I tell him I've just got back from sitting in on the first week of the Count Arthur Strong UK tour. Then I can't contain myself any longer and ask if he's had a chance to read the script. He clears his throat.

"Yeah I did yeah. I read it twice. It's very good actually. But we should make it a lot weirder, y'know what I'm saying?"

I know what he's saying. A month later, we do another couple of days on the script, working together in a room at the Midland Hotel in Manchester. Mark isn't above laughing at his own myth. He sits, smoking by the open window of the non-smoking room.

"In the recording studio we could look through my eyes, like fuckin' Terminator. Lookin' at the group, with data coming up: working out if I should fire 'em or not."

We burst out laughing, but in the end we decide against including it in the script. It feels like too much of a perception from the outside world – and we're trying to create our own world. When I get back to Brighton I print off the second draft and post it to Mark. We decide it's ready.

Perhaps inevitably, we encounter the same kinds of response as we did with the TV pitches. Mark's reputation for difficult and contrary behaviour seems to make companies nervous of committing to a project that would involve him both on screen and behind it. One film executive snootily informs me,

"Like everybody, I saw the interview he did when John Peel died. I didn't think it was very respectful, did you?"

"No, not really," I agree. "But I have to say, I think Peel would have been utterly delighted."

The other thing we seem to be hearing a lot is: "It's a bit too weird". And there was I thinking we'd got the weirdness level just right. These rejections are frustrating, but I don't take it to heart. I'm well aware there are a number of wonderful films whose scripts spent a decade or more kicking around offices, before being picked up. I tell Mark I think this might end up being one of those.

We continue to chat on the phone, we meet up for drinks whenever I'm in Manchester and I still see The Fall as often as I can. Then one day Mark phones up. After a short preamble, he informs me he's been diagnosed with lung cancer.

"Quite disappointing actually."

▲ ▲ ▲

Some of the scenes in the script are based on real events from Mark's life. The sequence where he and Jeff go to score weed at Nicholls's house was inspired by a story Mark told. As a young man he and a mate had gone to score some hash from a guy they'd never met before. He turned out to be a city councillor, who apparently answered the door stark naked. Upon inviting Mark and his mate inside, he proceeded to try and seduce them into some kind of swingers scenario with his middle-aged friends.

As Mark remarked: "Soon as we'd scored the hash we couldn't fuck off quick enough!"

Perhaps surprisingly, mayors and dignitaries minus trousers or underwear were a recurring feature of a number of Mark's stories from the 1970s – almost as if an element of the Brian Rix farces of that era had permeated his life. Naturally it felt right to include some of that in the script.

Mark was also fascinated by the Jacobite rebellion, and how a Jacobite victory could have led to the overthrow of the British Royal family, and changed the course of history. So the ghosts of Jacobite soldiers and their disruptive energies found their way into the story too.

The sequence where Mark encounters the ghosts was inspired by real life instances he recounted of visions of ancient spectral presences. He told me that the first time he visited the Haçienda nightclub he had visions of Victorian poorhouse children in chains. He claimed to have intermittently had visions and pre-cognitive experiences throughout his life. Again this felt like it easily earned its place in the narrative.

Once the character of Mary the folk singer came up, I started looking around for a song connected to the Jacobites. I found it in the old folk song 'Lo The Bird Has Fallen', which recounts the battle of Preston of 1715, when Jacobites and government forces clashed in the city streets and numerous buildings were burnt down. The fact the word *Fallen* appeared in the song's title made it all the more resonant, and so the lyrics were included within the script. Had the film gone into production, Mark had planned for The Fall to record some new songs and instrumentals for the soundtrack. A shame indeed, this didn't come to pass.

Oddly, a month or so after Mark died, during a phone call with Elena, she mentioned that they had previously written a film script together, entitled *The World Age 4*. She told me it was about animals taking over society. Initially it struck me as odd, that in all the time we'd spent working and talking together, Mark had never once mentioned this to me. Then I realised why. Mark *knew* that if he *had* referred to it, I would have been keen to read it and consider the possibilities of doing something with it. But that would be looking back. What Mark wanted to do, as ever, was to move forward and to create something fresh.

Although it was never made into a film, I'm still very proud of *The Otherwise* and all the work that went into it. As a script it may well be weird. But I honestly don't think it's "too weird". The irony is we always said that once we got the project into production there would be the opportunity to use editing and the visual language of film to take the material into much more abstracted territory – to essentially make it weirder.

Collaborating with Mark was a unique and thrilling experience. We were obviously very different people and I'm sure on occasion he found me too fussy, and I admit, his desire to keep everything in flux could be challenging. But he was a playful, generous and exhilarating creative partner.

Having been inspired by his imaginings since the age of 14, it was an honour and a solid hoot to be able to sit and dream up ideas together. If I were able to say one last thing to Mark, it would be "Cheers cock."

▲ ▲ ▲

THE OTHERWISE

An Original Feature Film

THE
OTHERWISE

An original feature film

Written by

MARK E. SMITH & GRAHAM DUFF

2nd Draft
April 23rd 2015

<u>EXT. - PENDLE HILL - NIGHT</u>

Initially the screen is completely black. Then white text appears, a line at a time:

> "Its truth was amazing.
> O Joy! Solaris-like!
> White and translucent foams.
> It squirmed unfettered.
> Energized in wondrous coil."
>
> — **Ian MacFisk**. *With the Jacobite Army in Lancashire 1746.*

As the text fades, we fade in on a WIDE SHOT of Pendle Hill, lit by a full moon. We hear the sound of a car engine.

A grubby white Honda Accord drives up the roadway.

CUT TO:

<u>INT. - BEV'S CAR - NIGHT</u>

BEV is driving. JEFF has the map open. JEFF (38) is handsome but slightly scrawny, unshaven and unsure of himself. BEV (33) is attractive, smart and fairly confident. But right now, BEV is irritated with JEFF. JEFF turns the map around.

BEV

Don't turn the map around. That doesn't help.

JEFF

It helps me. It helps me orientate myself.

BEV

So if you're oriented, how come we're lost?

JEFF

Hang on, hang on.

BEV

Use your mobile.

JEFF lifts his mobile. C.U. on the screen. Their position is a pulsing blue dot on a completely empty grid.

JEFF

It's still not loading.

BEV

For Christ's sake.

JEFF

I'm doing my best! You know I'm shit at map reading.

The increasingly irritated BEV drives the car into a stopping place.

CUT TO:

EXT. - HILLSIDE - NIGHT

The car pulls into the stopping place by a gate.

CUT TO:

INT. - BEV'S CAR - NIGHT

BEV takes the map and the mobile from JEFF.

BEV

Right, let me see if I can calmly and quietly sort this out.

JEFF

I think I'll stretch me legs.

CUT TO:

EXT. - HILLSIDE - NIGHT

JEFF gets out of the car, clambers over the gate, moves behind the wall and unzips his fly. He stands pissing as he surveys the landscape. He glances down at the ground.

C.U. on the muddy earth as the piss hits it. We see something glinting in the moonlight.

JEFF finishes pissing, crouches down and looks at the mud. C.U. on two silver coins.

JEFF picks them up and stands.

CUT TO UNKNOWN POV: Somebody is watching JEFF from behind some bushes about eight feet away.

JEFF takes out his mobile and uses its light to illuminate the coins in his palm.

E.C.U. on the ancient coins, on the heads side there are two faces.

CUT TO UNKNOWN POV: JEFF is still being watched, but now from only a few feet away. We can tell JEFF is in danger.

Suddenly we hear a loud motorbike approaching at speed. A moment later a BIKER roars past, his headlight momentarily illuminating JEFF and the nearby car. In an instant it's gone, the sound of the engine fading. JEFF pockets the coins, belatedly glancing behind him. There's no one there. JEFF clambers over the gate.

CUT TO:

INT. - BEV'S CAR - NIGHT

BEV is calmly massaging her temples. The passenger door opens and JEFF climbs back in the car. He gives BEV an uncertain smile. She returns a conciliatory smile.

BEV

It's okay. I'm not still angry.

(passes the map)

We're actually not far from your sister's place. I've marked the route in pencil.

JEFF looks at the route on the map.

JEFF
This looks idiot proof.

BEV
(pecks his cheek)
Let's find out shall we?

JEFF
Look what I found.
(passes her the coins)
I think they're Roman.

BEV examines the coins closely and shakes her head.

BEV
No.

JEFF
How can you be sure?

BEV
(chuckles)
They're dated 1693. The Romans were long gone by then.

JEFF
(points to heads)
Those two *look* Roman.

BEV
1693. That's William and Mary. You been digging?

JEFF
They were just lying on the ground in the field.

BEV

What, on the surface? Probably fakes then.

JEFF

We'll see. Let's get them valued. Put 'em in your purse.

BEV

(sniffs the coins)

Why do they smell of piss?

JEFF shrugs.

CUT TO:

EXT. - HILLSIDE - NIGHT

The Honda Accord pulls out onto the empty road and drives away.

PULL BACK TO REVEAL: Two men are watching the car. They are Scottish Jacobites. The first: IAN MACFISK is a young, thoughtful, skinny man. He wears a dark tartan kilt and tam o' shanter and an animal skin jerkin. The second man is ALUN MACREEDY. He's bigger and more ox-like. Not stupid but far from sophisticated. He wears a long coat and a tam o' shanter.

DISSOLVE TO:

EXT. - CLARE'S FARMHOUSE - NIGHT

A large farmhouse, with surrounding outhouses and a big converted cattle shed clustered around a large yard.

A sign reads "Otherwise Recording Studio".

The white Honda Accord comes up the road, turns up the drive.

CUT TO:

EXT. - YARD - CONTINUOUS

The car parks outside the farmhouse. A moment later, JEFF and BEV climb out. BEV admires the layout.

BEV

Nice.

The farmhouse door opens and CLARE steps out. She's 35 and pretty, but disguises this by dressing in very practical clothes and glasses. She's really pleased to see them.

CLARE

Hi!

CLARE and BEV hug.

CLARE (CONT'D)

Ooh so good to see you.

BEV

And you. Thanks for having us to stay.

CLARE and JEFF hug.

CLARE

Hi ya.

JEFF
You look very healthy and relaxed.

CLARE
Oh good. Well, join me.

CLARE tries to open their car boot, but it won't budge.

JEFF
There's a knack to it.

JEFF has a fiddle with the lock, but it still won't budge.

BEV
And unfortunately, you don't have it.

BEV fiddles with the lock and suddenly the boot pops open. At that moment, several things spill out, including a spade which lands heavily on CLARE's Doc Marten cladded foot.

CLARE
Ow!

BEV
Shit. Sorry.

CLARE
It's okay. Thank God for Docs.

BEV
I told Jeff "Just pack the stuff you can't bear to leave behind." Apparently that includes a spade.

JEFF
I'd just bought it. Was gonna do the garden. I can do your garden.

CLARE
(chuckles)
We haven't got a garden.

They begin carrying suitcases into the house.

CUT TO:

INT. - CLARE'S LOUNGE - NIGHT

It's 40 minutes later. The lighting is dimmed. CLARE and BEV are drinking red wine. JEFF swigs from a can of lager.

There is a wood burning stove, big old sofas, hippy rugs and some paintings of the local hillside. The mood is relaxed and convivial.

BEV
Don't get me wrong, we've had some great times but...

JEFF
We just need to be away from Manchester for a bit.

CLARE
So where you thinking of?

JEFF
Maybe towards Preston way? Not sure. Need to find some work first.

CLARE
Moving away was the best thing I ever did.

BEV
You've been talking about setting up a recording studio since I started seeing Jeff. Which is... nearly 5 years. So the fact you've actually made it happen... hats off to you Clare. You are one impressive lady.

BEV clinks her glass.

CLARE
Awh thanks sweetheart.

JEFF
Yeah, well done. It is pretty bloody cool.

CLARE
I'll take you over to see the studio in a bit.

JEFF
And can you attract bands out here? It is a bit out of the way.

CLARE
Doesn't seem to be a problem. Plus lots of musicians still like the idea of 'getting their head together in the countryside'.

BEV

It's so quiet. The city gets too noisy some times. After the break in I just couldn't relax. The slightest sound...

HARD CUT TO:

INT. - JEFF'S OLD FLAT - NIGHT (FLASHBACK)

The empty hallway of a modest flat in a shared block. A few coats on hooks. Gig posters on the walls. We hear the sound of a key in the front door. The door opens and a slightly drunken JEFF and BEV enter. JEFF closes the door and they kiss. Suddenly they hear a noise from the living room. BEV and JEFF exchange a concerned look. JEFF walks cautiously up to the closed living room door and opens it.

CUT TO:

INT. - JEFF'S OLD LIVING ROOM - CONTINUOUS

JEFF's POV: He pushes open the door to be confronted by the sight of two teenage SCALLIES. One has a laptop under his arm. The other has the flat screen TV. They turn to see JEFF.

JEFF

What the fuck?

The FIRST SCALLY with the laptop pulls out a Stanley knife and points it at JEFF!

1ST SCALLY

Keep the fuck away from us and we'll leave you alone.

JEFF

Okay. Okay.

A scared JEFF holds up his hands. He nods to the door indicating they should just go. At that moment, BEV appears in the doorway. Upon seeing the intruders and the knife she gives a little scream.

1ST SCALLY

Shut her up!

JEFF gently pulls BEV towards him and puts his hand over her mouth. BEV stifles her anxiety. The 1ST SCALLY nods for the 2ND SCALLY to go. He duly exits the room with the TV. The 1ST SCALLY walks slowly past them, pausing to hold the knife close to BEV's face.

1ST SCALLY (CONT'D)

Night then.

A second later and he's gone. We hear the front door slam shut. JEFF releases BEV. She's short of breath and pulls out her inhaler and takes a hit. JEFF's expression suggests he can scarcely believe what just happened.

CUT BACK TO:

INT. - CLARE'S LOUNGE - NIGHT

CLARE, JEFF and BEV are as we left them.

CLARE

Must have been terrifying.

BEV

Couldn't sleep for a week.
Thought I'd never sleep again.
Til Jeff snuck a couple of
sleeping pills in my lasagne.

CLARE

(joking)

Such a knight in shining armour.

They hear a loud motorbike pulling up outside.

CLARE (CONT'D)

That'll be Len.

JEFF

Sounds like a big bike.

CLARE

It is. Triumph Rocket 3. Len's
obsessed. He's a proper biker.
He's just joined this gang: The
Sons of Witches.

JEFF

(giggles)

That's a terrible name.

CLARE

Don't let Len catch you saying
that. Takes it very seriously.

BEV

(bemused)

So *how* did you meet him?

CLARE

He's a mechanic. Came to fix my car about three months back. We got drunk, somehow he never left.

JEFF

Fairy tale romance.

BEV

If it works it works.

CLARE

It *mainly* works.

JEFF

So has he got any baggage?

BEV

(chiding)

Jeff! Straight in there.

CLARE

What you mean kids or ex-wives?

JEFF

Yeah.

CLARE

No. I'm his first long term relationship.

BEV

Three months isn't *that* long term.

CLARE chuckles. Enter LEN (late 40's). He's tall and chunky with a shaven head and multiple earrings and a nose ring. He wears biker's leathers and is blunt and self-assured.

CLARE

Hi. Len, this is Bev and Jeff.

LEN comes into the room and shakes hands with BEV and JEFF.

BEV

Hi.

LEN

Alright?

JEFF

Nice to meet you mate.

LEN

Find the place ok?

BEV

(laughs)

Well, we *did* get lost. But that was largely due to the mapreader.

CLARE

(laughs)

Jeff's sense of direction has always been shit!

JEFF

I admit it. Give me a map and I only get *more* confused.

LEN

I'm gonna grab a beer. Anybody want anything from the kitchen?

They shake their heads and decline. LEN goes to the kitchen.

JEFF

How long did it take you to kit out the studio?

CLARE

It actually came together pretty quickly. Come on, I'll show you.

CLARE stands up, taking her glass of wine with her.

CUT TO:

EXT. - YARD - NIGHT

CLARE, JEFF and BEV walk across the yard to the outhouse buildings. There's a solid looking door with a light over it on the larger outhouse. CLARE unlocks the door, pushes it open and waves them in. The three of them disappear inside and the door closes.

CUT TO:

EXT. - FIELD - NIGHT

MACFISK and ALUN - the two Jacobites - are walking when they come in sight of Clare's farmhouse. They come to a halt and scrutinise the house.

MACFISK

I reckon this place'll do.

ALUN nods.

CUT TO:

INT. - STUDIO CONTROL ROOM - NIGHT

CLARE is showing JEFF and BEV around the studio. It's neat and organised, but it's noticeable that it isn't a digital set up. The mixing desk and almost all the equipment are analogue. There are also some 50's or 60's vintage mics and so on dotted about.

Through the window above the mixing desk we can see into a live room with valve amps.

CLARE

We've been up and running nearly six months now. And the bookings have been really good. We've had two or three days here and there with nothing going on, but to be honest, I've been rushed off my feet.

JEFF peers through the window into the live room.

JEFF

It's a big space.

CLARE

Used to be a cattle shed.

BEV

Does Len help in the studio?

CLARE

No. It's not his thing. Plus, I think he'd just get in the way.

JEFF

So what's the idea of not having any digital equipment?

CLARE

The idea is to get great sounding recordings. Valve amps, vintage mics, reel to reel. It's all so much more tangible. The sound you get in there is gorgeous.

BEV

Is it like a thing to attract like purists?

CLARE

There's a bit of that. But we get a real range of people coming in. Folk singers, blues bands, reggae group in last week. In fact, guess who's coming in for a week starting tomorrow.

JEFF

Who? The Who?

CLARE

The Fall.

JEFF

(impressed)

Seriously?

CLARE nods.

JEFF (CONT'D)

Shit. They're coming here tomorrow?

CLARE

Yep.

BEV

Jeff *loves* The Fall.

CLARE

I *know* he does. It was always blaring out of his room when we were growing up.

BEV

Tell me about it.

CLARE

Anyway, I spoke to Mark Smith on the phone and he's *really* into the all analogue set up. They're gonna record an EP here. And if that goes well, they might come back and do the next album. But y'know, one step at a time.

JEFF

Nice one.

BEV

I just need to nip and get my inhaler.

JEFF

(joking)

She's got all over excited about The Fall.

BEV smiles and heads out of the room.

INT. - CLARE'S LOUNGE - NIGHT

LEN switches on the TV and flicks to motor racing.

CUT TO:

He notices Bev's handbag by the side of the sofa. He picks it up and quickly sifts the contents; bunch of keys, address book, scraps of paper, a broach, pen, a couple of button badges, small pack of sanitary towels, lipsticks. He opens her purse, inside are a couple of ten pound notes and some change. He's about to close it when he spots the silver coins. He takes them out and turns them over in his hand.

CUT TO:

EXT. - YARD - NIGHT

BEV walks across the yard back to the house. She looks cold and vulnerable. Suddenly she notices something out of the corner of her eye.

MACFISK and ALUN are standing by the gateway, staring up at the house. BEV gives them an uncertain wave.

BEV

Hello?

Seemingly 'looking through' her, MACFISK and ALUN turn away from the house and walk on out of sight.

CUT TO:

INT. - CLARE'S LOUNGE - NIGHT

LEN is sitting on the sofa, swigging a can of lager and watching the motor racing on TV. BEV enters.

BEV

Hi. Is my bag in here?

LEN glances about in a half-hearted fashion.

LEN

Not sure.

BEV spots her handbag down by the side of the sofa.

BEV

Ah, here we go.

BEV picks up the bag and sits on the sofa. She pulls out her inhaler and takes a hit with a swift gasp. LEN glances over and smiles.

LEN

I like that sound.

BEV

Yeah?

LEN

Yeah.

Beat.

LEN (CONT'D)

Sounded like you were having an orgasm.

BEV is momentarily thrown by how casually predatory this is, but she quickly asserts herself.

BEV

Well I definitely wasn't.

LEN

How are things with you and the Jeffster then?

Having only just met LEN, BEV is unsure how open to be.

BEV

We erm. Things are great thanks. Really... solid.

LEN

That's nice.

BEV

How about you and Clare?

LEN

Clare?

LEN gets distracted by TV for a moment, before returning to the conversation.

LEN (CONT'D)

Clare's ace.

BEV

(smiles)

Yeah, she is.

LEN

Yeah.

Beat.

BEV

She said you came to fix the car.

LEN

Yep. Came for the Volvo stayed for the vulva.

BEV

(awkward laugh)

Right.

Beat.

LEN

You should see her naked. Fuckin' gorgeous. Shockingly decent tits.

Again BEV isn't sure how to react.

BEV

Nice for you both.

LEN

Bet you look hot in a bikini Bev.

BEV

(sarcastic)

Not as hot as you would I'm sure.

BEV stands and makes for the door.

LEN

Don't forget your orgasmatron.

LEN points at the sofa. BEV turns to see her inhaler on the sofa.

BEV

Thanks.

BEV pockets the inhaler. LEN returns his attention to the TV.

LEN

Be nice having you around.

BEV exits. LEN smiles to himself and returns to watching the TV.

CUT TO:

INT. - STUDIO CONTROL ROOM/STUDIO HALLWAY - NIGHT

As they talk, CLARE and JEFF exit the control room and walk down the hallway toward the front door.

CLARE

Bev looks tired.

JEFF

We both are. We need to recharge a bit. Thanks for this. You seem to have it pretty chilled here so...

CLARE

(joking)

Len has his unchilled moments. But he's out a lot anyway. Stay for longer than two weeks if you want. Seriously.

JEFF

We'll see. I'll paint that back room for you anyway.

CLARE

That'll be great.

CLARE opens the front door, then gasps at what she sees.

HARD CUT to an OCTOGENARIAN WOMAN's FACE staring at them. Her face is hard, wrinkled and sour. Cut to reveal she's dressed in a large, thick black overcoat and hat. She also carries a black acoustic guitar case.

CLARE (CONT'D)

Mary! Sorry I... I completely forgot you were booked in tonight.

CLARE stands aside and MARY enters carrying her guitar case. MARY smiles at JEFF.

MARY

Mary Tunstall.

CLARE

This is Jeff. My brother.

MARY nods at JEFF.

JEFF

You a musician Mary?

MARY

Aye. Singer. I like to record the old, old songs. Stops 'em getting forgotten.

CLARE

Go through Mary. I'll get everything sorted out for you.

MARY shuffles down the hallway towards the studio. JEFF watches her go.

CUT TO:

INT. - STUDIO CONTROL ROOM - NIGHT

GRAMS: 'LO! THE BIRD IS FALLEN'.

We hear acoustic guitar playing coming through from the live room. CLARE is setting levels. JEFF is sitting sipping a beer and watching how CLARE works.

DISSOLVE TO:

INT. - LIVE ROOM - NIGHT

GRAMS: (CONTINUE).

MARY sits in front of a couple of mics playing her guitar. Her eyes are closed. She plays as if in a trance. She begins to sing.

MARY

(sings)

Three cheers for Edward Jolly,
Who fought a doughty fight!
When the rebels from Preston,
He drove in headlong flight.

DISSOLVE TO:

EXT. - YARD - NIGHT

GRAMS: (CONTINUE).

The yard is empty. All lights are off in the house. The only light comes from the full moon.

MARY (V.O.)
(sings)
From the fleet at Marton,
In aid of good King George,
He marched with Cotton's Regiment,
A victory to forge.

DISSOLVE TO:

EXT. - HILLSIDE - NIGHT

GRAMS: (CONTINUE).

We move across the empty fields.

MARY (V.O.)
(sings)
With pride he bore his
fowling piece,
Against whose cannonade,

EXT. - WOODS - NIGHT

GRAMS: (CONTINUE).

DISSOLVE TO:

We move through trees in the dark woods, occasional patches of moonlight illuminate the ground.

MARY (V.O.)
(sings)
No duck, no goose, no rebel,
Might raise a barricade.

DISSOLVE TO:

EXT. - WELL SPRING - NIGHT

GRAMS: (CONTINUE).

We move to a clearing. There's a well spring, gently gurgling. The water begins to glow - gently at first - then with an increasingly bright white light. Something very strange is happening.

MARY (V.O.)
(sings)
In town the traitor Mayfield,
In defiance gave no quarter,

LEN steps into view. He stares at the well spring with a slightly sneering expression. He pulls something from his pocket.

C.U. on the two silver coins in the palm of his hand.

MARY (V.O.)
(sings)
When troops of Wills and Carpenter,
He fired upon in slaughter.

LEN tosses one coin into the glowing water.

F/X SHOT: The coin seems to land on the surface of the glowing white water. It glows a bright red then seems to dissolve into the water.

LEN tosses in the next coin. The same thing happens. LEN shakes his head, seemingly disappointed.

As he watches, the water glows brighter and brighter.

WHITE OUT:

FADE IN:

INT. - SPARE ROOM - NIGHT

GRAMS: (CONTINUE).

BEV is sitting up in bed in the spare room. It's a decent size but looks a little unloved, with some spare bits and pieces stashed to one side. The room is illuminated only by a bedside lamp. BEV applies her moisturizer from a small jar. She finishes then switches off the lamp and snuggles down into the bedding. A moment later JEFF enters. He assumes she's asleep and quietly slips out of his clothes and into bed. They lie together silently for a moment.

GRAMS: (DIP TO BED).

BEV
What do you think of Len?

JEFF
Erm. I dunno. He's not like any of her other boyfriends. What do you think of him?

BEV
I don't like him. I dislike him.

JEFF
Why?

BEV
The way he does things, the way he says things. Stuff like that.

JEFF
That's pretty comprehensive
disliking.

Beat.

BEV
I'm not sure about staying here.

JEFF
Give it a chance. It won't be for
long. Clare says Len's out most
of the time anyway.

BEV
That'd be good.

GRAMS: (SWELL).

They lie silently together in the darkened room.

CUT TO:

EXT. - CLARE'S FARMHOUSE - MORNING

GRAMS: THE FALL - 'LOADSTONES' (00:00).

CUT TO:

Establishing shot. A large van drives up and in
through the gateway.

CUT TO:

EXT. - YARD - MORNING

GRAMS: (CONTINUE).

The van pulls up. A moment later, THE FALL climb out of the van: KIERON is the close cropped and muscular drummer, PETER the guitarist is lean and wiry, ELENA the keyboardist is dark haired, pretty and elfin, DAVE is the handsome bearded bassist.

CLARE comes out of the studio to greet them.

GRAMS: (DIP TO BED).

CLARE
Hi, I'm Clare. Nice to meet you.

ELENA
Elena. Hi.

They shake hands.

ELENA (CONT'D)
Are we okay to just start bringing things in?

CLARE
Yeah sure.

CUT TO:

INT. - LIVE ROOM - DAY

KEIRON is putting his drum kit together. PETER is tuning up. DAVE is stringing his bass and ELENA is setting up her keyboard. They are chatting and CLARE is positioning various mic stands etc.

CUT TO:

INT. - KITCHEN - DAY

BEV is doing the washing up. JEFF is drying.

BEV
I didn't sleep that brilliantly last night.

JEFF
I was out like a light.

BEV
Yeah. A loud, snorey light.

BEV rinses the last piece of crockery and pulls the plug. JEFF still has quite a bit of drying to do. LEN enters. He's wearing overalls and his hands are dirty from working on his bike.

BEV (CONT'D)
Hi.

LEN
Morning.

JEFF
A'right? We were wondering if there was much of interest round here.

LEN
Interest?

BEV
Places to go and see.

LEN

No.

(snorts)

There's the well spring.

BEV

Oh lovely.

LEN

The water's ice cold. In the 18th century it produced wondrous things. It's supposed to protect the land.

JEFF

Yeah?

LEN

But the locals abused it for sexual pleasure. The drumming up of angel babes for the infertile.

JEFF is uncertain how to respond.

BEV

Sounds like an afternoon out. Right, I'm gonna see if Clare needs any help in the studio.

JEFF

Hark at Phil Spector.

BEV smiles and exits.

LEN

Very tasty.

JEFF

Uh?

LEN

Your Bev, very tasty.

JEFF

(nods awkwardly)

Yeah. She's lovely.

LEN

Bev told Clare that you're a good mate of this Mark E. Smith feller.

JEFF is a little awkward.

JEFF

Not exactly a *mate*. Been to a lot of Fall gigs. I've met him two or three times in Manchester.

LEN

So you lied to her?

JEFF

No, you know what it's like when you meet a girl - trying to impress - we all do it! I know him to say hello to like. Why, have you got tapes or music to pass on?

LEN

(with scorn)

Taaapes? Music?

LEN shakes his head. JEFF goes to fill the kettle.

LEN (CONT'D)
Can I ask you something serious Jeff?

JEFF tries to lighten the mood.

JEFF
Sure, potential bro-in-law.

LEN
Did he send you here?

JEFF
What? Who?

LEN
Smith.

JEFF
(genuinely confused)
What? No! What d'yer mean?

LEN
Is he 'prezzy'?

JEFF
(uncertain)
Does that mean cracked round 'ere like?

LEN
No! Answer. Is he prezzy?

JEFF
From Preston?

LEN
Pres-by-terian.

JEFF
Oh. No. Not as far as I know.

LEN grunts.

JEFF (CONT'D)
Is that important? Are you... religious?

LEN
(snorts)
I'm a Son of a Witch. We have our own beliefs.

JEFF
What er... what are they then?

LEN looks at him for a moment then changes the subject and seems suddenly friendly.

LEN
You like bikes yeah?

JEFF
Erm, yeah.

LEN
Good.

CUT TO:

EXT. - WOODS - DAY

MACFISK and ALUN are walking slowly through the woods. They are tired. Their spirits low.

MACFISK
I'm cold.

Beat.

ALUN

I'm *fuckin'* cold.

They walk on.

ALUN (CONT'D)

Fuckin' Lancashire.

MACFISK

Wish I were with the main army
in Preston.

ALUN

I dunno. At least we're safe here.

MACFISK

(annoyed)

I didnae sign up to be *safe*! I
did it coz I wanna see a Stuart
King back on the throne!

ALUN

Aye, aye.

They walk on.

MACFISK

But the deeds expected of us...

ALUN

Hm?

MACFISK

Well it's no like fightin'.
It's...

ALUN

It's what?

MACFISK

It's just devilment.

ALUN

Aye. Forster said he wanted us to make chaos.

MACFISK gives a weary shake of his head as they walk on.

ALUN (CONT'D)

See me, I nae had an education. Nae fit frae ought much. But *chaos*? Aye, I can do *that*.

MACFISK and ALUN walk on.

CUT TO:

INT. - LIVE ROOM - DAY

GRAMS: THE FALL - 'INSTRUMENTAL 1' (00.00).

ELENA, PETER, DAVE and KIERON are playing an instrumental track.

CUT TO:

INT. - STUDIO CONTROL ROOM - DAY

GRAMS: (CONTINUE).

CLARE is listening to the band and adjusting levels etc. BEV brings in a tray of coffees.

BEV
How's it going?

CLARE
Sounding great yeah.

BEV
How do you know about all this stuff?

CLARE
All what? The equipment?
(chuckles)
Um, it's a bit like your TV remote. Hundreds of buttons but you only need to *know* what a few of them do.

BEV
Yeah, but not just the machines. I mean how do you know about music full stop? I mean, I like music, but I don't know about it.

CLARE
To be honest with you, I can't really hold a tune, I can't properly play an instrument. But, I do know what sounds good, I know what sounds right.

BEV
Do blokes in bands treat you differently coz you're a woman?

CLARE
Sometimes. Not this lot. That's another reason why it's best if Len doesn't help.

BEV

What d'yer mean?

CLARE

Well if there's a bloke in here. People start acting as if *he's* the boss and *I'm* the assistant.

BEV

Of course. Of course.

GRAMS: (SWELL).

CUT TO:

EXT. - COUNTRY ROAD - DAY

A dark blue car is driving along the road.

CUT TO:

INT. - ED'S CAR - DAY

MARK E. SMITH is in the passenger seat. The driver is his mate ED - early 40s and matter-of-fact.

MARK

How much further?

ED

Not far. Wouldn't have thought this was you.

MARK

What?

ED

Recording in the countryside.

MARK
Could be okay. What you've got to remember is once the group are inside a recording studio it doesn't matter where it is. Coz they're not coming out 'til the fucking job is done.

MARK and ED chuckle.

CUT TO:

INT. - GARAGE - DAY

CUT TO:

LEN is working on his motorbike. The garage door creaks open and JEFF enters. LEN looks up, his expression unreadable.

JEFF
Alright? Need a hand?

LEN
Just tinkering with the engine.

Beat.

JEFF
So you're a proper Hell's Angel then?

LEN
(snorts)
What's that mean?

JEFF

I dunno. Do you drink chicken's blood or –

LEN

(firmly)

– We're the Sons of Witches. And we don't discuss what we do with outsiders.

JEFF

Right.

An awkward moment. JEFF looks around the garage.

LEN

You're into bikes then?

JEFF

Er yeah. Never had anything like this though.

(nods to Len's bike)

I used to ride a Kawasaki. Then sold it when I got skint.

LEN pulls a dust sheet off another motorbike - a Harley Davidson.

LEN

Reckon you could handle this?

JEFF

(admiringly)

I'd definitely like to give it a go.

LEN

Take it out tonight. We'll have a bomb 'round Pendle.

JEFF

Nice one. Yeah, love to.

JEFF kneels down and looks admiringly at the motorbike.

LEN looks down at the back of the kneeling JEFF. We can tell LEN is sizing him up and judging him as weak.

CUT TO:

EXT. - YARD - DAY

Ed's car pulls up into the yard. The passenger door opens and MARK gets out.

ED

Right, I'm off to Preston. See you later yeah?

MARK

A'right pal, see yer.

The car reverses out of the yard. As MARK lights a cigarette, something catches his eye. Over the wall, in an adjacent field, he can see MACFISK and ALUN staring over at the farmhouse.

MARK stares at them for a moment, then turns and walks towards the studio.

CUT TO:

EXT. - FIELD - DAY

MACFISK and ALUN stand watching.

ALUN

Well then?

MACFISK ponders a moment then shakes his head.

MACFISK

We should come back later. Do it after night fall.

ALUN

Why not now?

MACFISK

It's easier to make chaos at night. Folk are less sure of 'emselves. The darkness...

CUT TO:

EXT. - HILLSIDE - EVENING

ESTABLISHING SHOT of empty fields and dry stone walls. It's dusk. We see MARY, the octogenarian folk singer, shuffling along. She enters a wooded area.

CUT TO:

EXT. - WELL SPRING - EVENING

As the light fades from the sky, we move into C.U. on the gently bubbling waters of the well spring.

CUT TO REVEAL MARY watching the waters, thoughtful and focussed.

When the sunlight is finally gone, the water in the well spring begins to gently glow with light. MARY smiles. Despite the strangeness, MARY seems reassured. She closes her eyes and appears to enter a trance like state.

CUT TO:

INT. - LIVE ROOM - DAY

GRAMS: THE FALL - 'NEW SONG' (00.00).

MARK is watching THE FALL playing a new song.

CUT TO:

INT. - LIVE ROOM - DAY

GRAMS: (CONTINUE AS BED).

CLARE is at the mixing desk, checking the sound levels. BEV is sitting, going through her handbag.

BEV

That's odd.

CLARE

Hmm?

BEV

I was gonna show you these two coins Jeff found on the way here. Proper antiques; William and Mary.

CLARE

Would they be worth anything?

BEV

I thought they might be real silver. *If* I could find them.

BEV continues to search through her handbag.

CUT TO:

EXT. - PENDLE HILL - NIGHT

GRAMS: (CONTINUE).

LEN and JEFF are riding the motorbikes. LEN is going at high speed. JEFF is struggling to keep up with him. LEN wears a black helmet with a reflective silver visor. JEFF wears a more ordinary helmet.

CUT TO:

EXT. - ROUGH TRACK - NIGHT

LEN drives off the road into the entrance to a rough track. He slides to a halt spraying gravel. Moments later, JEFF appears around the corner on his bike. He almost misses the turn off, but swerves and pulls up next to LEN. When they speak their voices are muffled.

LEN
(gestures down track)
This way.

JEFF
What's dow---

Before JEFF can finish speaking, LEN has roared away down the track. JEFF drives after him.

CUT TO:

EXT. - ABANDONED BARN - NIGHT

Six motorbikes are parked up in front of the dilapidated barn. LEN and JEFF pull up. LEN dismounts and heads inside. JEFF dismounts, takes off his helmet and follows him.

JEFF

What's happening here then?

LEN doesn't answer but simply disappears inside.

CUT TO:

INT. - ABANDONED BARN - CONTINUOUS

JEFF's POV: He follows LEN through the barn door inside.

It's very dark inside. The dark corners of the barn are impenetrable. But the very centre of the space is illuminated by three Tilley lamps. JEFF puts his hand on LEN's shoulder.

JEFF

Len?

LEN turns around and stares at him with his blank silver visor.

JEFF (CONT'D)

What's going on?

When LEN speaks his voice is muffled.

LEN

This is your chance.

JEFF
My chance?

LEN
(hisses)
Your chance to become a Son of a Witch.

JEFF
But I never said...

LEN grabs JEFF by the shoulder and pulls him forwards.

LEN
Come on. There's something you have to see.

LEN points to the lamps.

FOUR BIKERS in leathers and silver reflective visored helmets step forwards into the light. They stand facing inwards towards the light.

JEFF looks unsettled.

CUT TO:

INT. - STUDIO CONTROL ROOM - NIGHT

CLARE is at the mixing desk. She presses record. C.U. on the spool of tape turning on a reel to reel recorder. CLARE speaks into the mic.

CLARE
Okay, recording.

CUT TO:

INT. - LIVE ROOM - NIGHT

ELENA, PETER, DAVE and KIERON are at their instruments, MARK near the mic. The band start up. The music is slow, strange, ghostly and mysterious.

GRAMS: THE FALL - 'SOLARIS-LIKE' (00:00).

DISSOLVE TO:

INT. - ABANDONED BARN - NIGHT

GRAMS: (CONTINUE).

LEN and the other FOUR BIKERS are gathered in a circle around the uneasy JEFF. LEN and the BIKERS all have their helmets on and silver reflective visors down. They all join hands. The circle is complete. The nervous JEFF licks his lips. He makes a desperate bid to defuse the atmosphere.

JEFF

So then, what exactly are we doing? I'm er, I'm not sure what you want me to do. Just tell me and then...

(nervous laugh)

I'm presuming I'm not being sacrificed.

Suddenly, there's a tiny, but bright flicker of yellow light down on the ground by his feet. JEFF looks down, transfixed by the light.

DISSOLVE TO:

INT. - LIVE ROOM - NIGHT

GRAMS: (CONTINUE).

The unsettling music continues to play. The mood is more like a séance then a recording session. MARK intones into the mic.

MARK

It's truth was amazing. O Joy! Solaris-like! White and translucent foams. It squirmed unfettered, energised in wondrous coil.

DISSOLVE TO:

INT. - ABANDONED BARN - NIGHT

GRAMS: (CONTINUE).

F/X SHOT: The light continues to glow and increase in size. The light becomes a sphere of flames.

F/X SHOT: Suddenly the bristles of a broomstick appear next to the sphere of flames. A moment later, the whole broomstick is there. It appears to be trying to put out or brush away the flames. Yet this only spreads the flames across the ground.

JEFF looks on in awe. He's transfixed.

F/X SHOT: The broomstick becomes more agitated. Suddenly an OLD WOMAN appears. She's holding the broom and desperately waving it around. Suddenly the broom is in flames!

Suddenly the OLD WOMAN is in flames! The OLD WOMAN's wizened face contorts into a silent scream. JEFF recoils, but is somehow unable to step away.

CUT TO:

EXT. - FIELD - NIGHT

GRAMS: (CONTINUE).

MACFISK and ALUN stand with flaming torches. MACFISK holds one, ALUN has two. MACFISK winces and gives his head a slight shake.

GRAMS: (DIP TO BED).

ALUN
What's wrong wi' you?

MACFISK
That noise. Can you nae hear it?

ALUN
(strains)
Aye. Aye, what *is* that?

MACFISK
I dunno. It's weird. Almost like music.

CUT TO:

INT. - LIVE ROOM - NIGHT

GRAMS: (CONTINUE).

The sound of THE FALL grinds on, strange and unsettling.

CUT TO:

INT. - ABANDONED BARN - NIGHT

GRAMS: (CONTINUE).

E.C.U. on the OLD WOMAN's screaming burning face!

CUT TO:

EXT. - FIELD - NIGHT

GRAMS: (CONTINUE).

CUT TO:

MACFISK and ALUN stand holding their torches. They know what they must do, but both are hesitant.

ALUN

I suppose we'd best...

MACFISK nods. They move forward a few paces, but both begin to wince at the noise in their heads. They cannot walk any closer to the house, something is holding them back.

MACFISK

I cannae do it.

ALUN

What is it? What's stopping us?

MACFISK and ALUN try a moment longer. Their faces set, urging themselves to move towards the farmhouse. It's useless.

CUT TO:

INT. - STUDIO CONTROL ROOM - NIGHT

GRAMS: (CONTINUE).

The strange, ghostly music continues to play. CLARE is at the mixing desk. She seems to be almost in a trance.

Suddenly she gasps in fear at something she has seen in her mind's eye.

HARD CUT TO:

EXT. - FIELD - NIGHT

GRAMS: (CONTINUE).

MACFISK and ALUN running in fear away from the farmhouse, holding their flaming torches and fleeing through the darkness.

HARD CUT TO:

INT. - ABANDONED BARN - NIGHT

GRAMS: (CONTINUE).

Suddenly the light, the flames and the Witch disappear in an instant. JEFF blinks, then collapses in a faint.

HARD CUT TO:

INT. - LIVE ROOM - NIGHT

GRAMS: (CONTINUE).

The track concludes.

CUT TO:

INT. - STUDIO CONTROL ROOM - NIGHT

C.U. on the reel to reel tape recorder as the spools continue to spin.

HARD CUT TO:

INT. - CLARE'S LOUNGE - NIGHT

JEFF and LEN are drinking cans of lager. LEN seems at ease, whilst JEFF is clearly unsettled by the vision he saw in the barn. LEN clinks his can.

LEN

Now you've seen the witch, you're one of us. A Son of a Witch.

JEFF

Is she really a witch?

LEN

She's on fire and she's waving a broomstick around! It's as conclusive as fuck. This is *Pendle* mate.

JEFF

I'm still shaking.

LEN

I know. Shat meself when I first saw her. Literally. Only a little bit, but still. Proper terrifying.

LEN clinks his can against JEFF's can.

LEN (CONT'D)
Welcome brother.

LEN takes a confident swig. JEFF takes a nervous sip. LEN points to his own silver visored helmet on the sofa.

LEN (CONT'D)
You'll need to get yourself a proper helmet. I'll warn you, they're not cheap.

JEFF
So what do you do?

LEN
What d'yer mean?

JEFF
What do you - as a bike gang - actually do?

LEN
Well y'know. Drive around, have a few beers, watch porn, do a bit o' speed.

JEFF
Jesus, I haven't had any speed since I was about 18. But, but that's it?

LEN
What d'yer mean?

JEFF
You don't do anything else? Surely the Witch must *give* you something?

LEN shrugs.

JEFF (CONT'D)
See I thought contact with these sort of spirits was supposed to give you power, influence and... dominion? Otherwise what's the poin---

JEFF stops mid sentence as the door creaks open. It's BEV. She loiters in the doorway, without make-up and dressed in pajamas.

BEV
Thought I could hear your voice.

JEFF
Hi love. All right?

BEV
Yeah. Just can't sleep. You okay? You look pale.

JEFF
No I'm, I'm sound.
(indicates can)
I'll just finish this then I'll be up.

BEV
Okay. See you in a bit. Night Len.

LEN
Night Bev.

BEV exits closing the door. Beat. JEFF looks at LEN.

JEFF
(lowers his voice)
Think she heard anything?

LEN
(shakes his head)
And make sure she never does. Sons of Witches don't tell anyone else their business.

JEFF
(joking)
Like what kind of porn you watch, or what beer you drink?

LEN suddenly grabs JEFF by the throat. JEFF gasps.

LEN
(threatening whisper)
We don't fuckin' joke about this stuff pal! We don't joke about it. We don't discuss it with outsiders. And we *never* talk about the Witch. Not even to Bev. I don't tell Clare. Understood?

JEFF nods. LEN releases him.

LEN (CONT'D)
Good. So hopefully I won't have to do that again.

JEFF rubs his neck.

JEFF
Okay, okay. Sorry.

LEN

Now if I were you, I'd go upstairs and give Bev a proper seeing to.

JEFF

(pretends to play along)

Right, yeah. Yeah, good idea.

LEN

That's obviously why she came down here. Wants it in every hole by the looks of her.

JEFF finds this offensive but due to his fear of LEN, he still half plays along.

JEFF

I'll er, see what I can do.

(stands up)

I'll catch you in the morning.

LEN

Let me know if you need any help with her. Very 'appy to join in.

(oily smile)

Sons of Witches share everything. I reckon Bev'd love that an' all.

JEFF

(increasingly awkward)

No, no she definitely wouldn't. Thanks anyway. See you tomorrow yeah?

JEFF can't get out of the room quick enough.

LEN

Night brother.

The door closes. LEN smiles to himself and swigs from his can.

DISSOLVE TO:

INT. - SPARE ROOM - NIGHT

OVERHEAD SHOT looking down at JEFF and BEV in bed. BEV is curled up, fast asleep. JEFF is wide awake and worried, staring up at the ceiling.

C.U. on JEFF's worried face.

JUMP CUT TO:

INT. - ABANDONED BARN - NIGHT (FLASHBACK)

The burning WITCH's face is silently screaming.

JUMP CUT TO:

INT. - SPARE ROOM - NIGHT

The troubled JEFF closes his eyes and cuddles up to BEV.

DISSOLVE TO:

EXT. - WOODS - NIGHT

MACFISK and ALUN are walking through the woods.

MACFISK

Here we are.

MACFISK points. A hundred yards or so away we can just make out a small fire in amongst the trees. There are FOUR JACOBITES sitting or standing around it.

CUT TO:

EXT. - WOODS - NIGHT

The JACOBITES are gathered around the bonfire warming themselves. They look grizzled and tired, their features illuminated in the darkness like faces in a Caravaggio painting.

They are: PATRICK (40), a burly fat man with a beard. DOUGLAS (32), a handsome ginger man. DAVIE (20), a strong, stocky man and ARTHUR (35), a small and balding man with a wiry frame. ARTHUR also wears a pair of spectacles with a large crack crossing the left lens. MACFISK and ALUN walk up to join them. PATRICK nods at them in greeting.

PATRICK

Evening lads.

ALUN

A'right?

MACFISK

(sniffs the air)

What's to eat?

DOUGLAS

All gone I'm afraid.

MACFISK

What?

ALUN
Yer didnae wait? Yer didnae think to save us some?

PATRICK
Thought you might not be coming.

MACFISK
We agreed to meet here.

DOUGLAS
You didnae turn up.

MACFISK
We've turned up now!

DAVIE
Too late.

MACFISK
Aye. But *why* is it too late?

PATRICK
Coz all the food is gone.

Beat.

ARTHUR
I have an apple you can share.

ARTHUR produces an apple from an inside pocket then pulls out a knife.

ALUN
An *apple*?

ARTHUR
Half an apple. Each.

ALUN flops down by the bonfire.

ALUN

Aye go on.

ARTHUR slices the apple in half, then offers half to MACFISK. MACFISK stares at it for a moment then takes it. ARTHUR passes the other half to ALUN. MACFISK bites into it and pulls a face.

MACFISK

Damn! That's tart!

ARTHUR

Aye. Reckon it's a cooking apple.

The other men chuckle. The infuriated MACFISK throws the apple half into the fire. It sprays up sparks then hisses loudly in amongst the red glowing logs.

CUT TO:

EXT. - CLARE'S FARMHOUSE - DAY

GRAMS: SOUND OF BAND REHEARSING.

Establishing shot of the building and out houses.

CUT TO:

INT. - STUDIO CONTROL ROOM - DAY

GRAMS: TRACK FOUR by THE FALL.

Through the window, we can see the band tuning up etc.

CLARE is threading a tape onto the reel to reel recorder. Through the glass we can see the band running through a number. MARK is sitting on the sofa, sorting through some hand written sheets of A4 paper.

JEFF comes in with a tray of coffees. JEFF is a little star struck by MARK, but he does his best to hide it.

JEFF

Hi Mark.

MARK

A'right.

JEFF

Jeff. I'm Clare's sister. Brother! We've met a few times before. After gigs and that.

MARK

Oh right yeah, I remember. How are you?

JEFF

Yeah I'm all right thanks. You?

MARK

Very good actually.

JEFF

Great.

JEFF passes a coffee to CLARE.

JEFF (CONT'D)

There you go.

CLARE

Thanks love.

JEFF stands awkwardly for a moment. He wants to talk further, but MARK has returned to looking through his lyric notes. JEFF makes for the door. MARK looks up.

MARK

Jeff?

JEFF pauses and turns around.

JEFF

Yeah?

MARK

You don't know where we can get any whizz do you?

JEFF

Speed? Erm, yeah, I might actually.

MARK smiles.

CUT TO:

EXT. - FIELD - DAY

A small HERD of COWS are gathered around a large metal feeding trough, munching on feed.

CUT TO WIDE SHOT: MACFISK and ALUN stand watching.

ALUN

Yer ganna do it then or what?

MACFISK

Aye. Aye I am.

MACFISK approaches the COWS cautiously. He slips between a couple of them and pushes his way to the edge of the trough. He reaches into his satchel and pulls out a handful of white pellets and tosses them in with the feed. Then another handful.

C.U. on the COWS munching the pellets in with the feed.

MACFISK struggles to get away from between the tightly packed COWS but finally manages it.

MACFISK (CONT'D)

Does nae seem right.

ALUN

What?

MACFISK

These lassies are blameless. They shouldnee have to suffer.

ALUN

Animals do nae suffer man. They live, they die.

MACFISK

Sure everything suffers. Only thing ye need fae sufferin' is being alive in the first place.

ALUN

Too late to worry now.

MACFISK and ALUN watch as the COWS munch on the pellets and the feed.

PULL FOCUS TO REVEAL a distant FIGURE watching them from the other side of the dry stone wall at the far edge of the field.

CUT TO REVEAL it's MARY the old folk singer. She stands watching them, in her hand is her guitar case. She shakes her head and walks away down the road. As she does so she begins to whistle the refrain from 'Lo! The Bird Has Fallen'.

CUT TO MACFISK and ALUN by the COWS. They react to the sound of the distant whistling as if to an incredibly loud piercing noise. Both men wince and plug their ears with their fingers. The sound is overpowering. MACFISK falls to his knees in pain.

HARD CUT TO:

INT. - LIVE ROOM - DAY

GRAMS: THE FALL - 'INSTRUMENTAL 2' (00:00).

THE FALL are playing.

After a couple of minutes, the sound of a revving motorbike engine fades in and drowns out the music

CUT TO:

INT. - GARAGE - DAY

The engine sound continues. C.U. on a motorbike engine.

CUT TO REVEAL LEN standing with the bike. He's revving the engine and listening to it. After a moment, the garage door opens and JEFF enters. LEN sees him but continues to rev the engine for a few moments longer. Finally he stops.

JEFF

All right?

LEN

(grunts)

Aye. Just listening.

JEFF stands admiring the bike.

JEFF

Beautiful machine.

LEN

I know. When you getting your own bike then? Can't be a Son of a Witch without a bike.

JEFF

Soon as I get some cash.

LEN

And your helmet.

JEFF

Yeah, sure. Mark asked if there was anywhere to get some speed. And I thought you might erm, have some leads?

LEN

Course. I'll just make a call.

LEN takes out his mobile taps at it, puts it to his ear and waits. After a moment he hears someone pick up.

LEN (CONT'D)
Can I speak to Councillor
Nicholls please?

LEN waits a moment. JEFF looks on a little bemused.

LEN (CONT'D)
Evening Councillor, it's Len.
Yeah, not bad. You got any
speed? Great ta. Yeah, a mate o'
mine'll be over to pick it up.
Thanks Councillor.

LEN pockets his mobile.

LEN (CONT'D)
Sorted.

JEFF
A Councillor? Wow. Thanks.

LEN
No problem. Anything for a fellow
Son of a Witch.

JEFF gives LEN a semi-relaxed smile.

CUT TO:

EXT. - COUNTRY ROAD - NIGHT

The Honda Accord is driving around the darkened roads. We see JEFF and MARK through the windows.

CUT TO:

INT. - BEV'S CAR - NIGHT

JEFF is driving, MARK is in the passenger seat.

MARK
A councillor? Selling speed?

JEFF
That's what Len says.

MARK
Doesn't surprise me to be honest.
He's probably just supplementing
his wages.

Beat.

JEFF
I remember when I were a kid,
I used to think grown ups were
always good. Never did owt wrong.

JEFF shakes his head.

JEFF (CONT'D)
Turns out we all do stuff that's
wrong pretty much every day.

MARK
What you going on about?

JEFF
Sorry. Nothing.

They drive on.

CUT TO:

EXT. - COUNTRY HOUSE - NIGHT

A large detached, double fronted Victorian house, set back from the road with a short gravel drive. The car drives in through the gateway and up to the house. There's a BMW parked up outside.

MARK and JEFF get out of the car and walk up the marble steps. JEFF rings the doorbell. After a couple of seconds, the porch light comes on. A moment later, the door opens to reveal NICHOLLS. He's late 30's, seriously overweight and balding with a dark beard and glasses. In one hand he has a can of lager, in the other a cigar. And, apart from a chunky gold watch, he's also completely naked. JEFF is slightly taken aback. MARK appears unruffled.

NICHOLLS

Well?

JEFF

Councillor Nicholls?

NICHOLLS

I have that honour.

MARK

Apparently you can sort out some whizz for us?

NICHOLLS

Not a problem gentlemen.
In you come.

NICHOLLS steps to one side and waves them in. JEFF and MARK walk inside.

CUT TO:

INT. - NICHOLLS'S LOUNGE - NIGHT

MARK and JEFF enter, the naked NICHOLLS follows them. JEFF can't help raising an eyebrow at the sight which greets them. The large room is decorated and furnished in the way one would expect of a wealthy Tory councillor's country house.

JACK (18) a lad in skater wear is sitting with headphones on, playing a violent video game on the wide screen TV.

There's DIANE - a large middle aged woman on the sofa. She wears sensible clothes and is knitting a scarf.

There are also two glamorous ESCORT GIRLS dressed only in lingerie who are chopping out lines on a 12" album sleeve on the coffee table. It seems like DIANE and JACK are oblivious to the ESCORT GIRLS. No one looks up to acknowledge MARK and JEFF.

NICHOLLS

This is Diane.

MARK

A'right love.

DIANE looks up, gives a brief nod and returns to knitting.

NICHOLLS

That there's our Jack.

The oblivious JACK continues playing his game.

NICHOLLS (CONT'D)
(gestures to girls)
And this is Natalie and... Sheena?

1ST ESCORT GIRL
Shareena.

JEFF
Hello.

MARK
A'right girls?

2ND ESCORT GIRL
Hi.

The ESCORT GIRLS smile at them.

NICHOLLS
Make yourselves at home gents.

JEFF takes a seat next to DIANE and MARK sits in an armchair. NICHOLLS goes over to the ESCORT GIRLS and snorts a line. MARK lights a cigarette. JEFF looks uncomfortable.

CUT TO:

INT. - SPARE ROOM - NIGHT

BEV is changing the bedding on the bed. She shakes out a big bed sheet. A knock at the door.

BEV
Come in.

LEN enters. BEV doesn't want to see him but conceals this.

BEV (CONT'D)

Hi.

LEN

What you up to?

BEV gestures semi-sarcastically to the sheets.

BEV

Changing the sheets.

LEN

I'll give you a hand.

LEN closes the door and walks over.

BEV

No, it's fine.

LEN

Let me help you.

BEV

Honestly, you don't have to.

LEN

Seriously, I think you could benefit from some help in the bedroom.

BEV

(suddenly tough)

What?

LEN

Come on. The walls aren't that thick here. I would of heard if you and wonder boy had done any shagging.

BEV

That what you into is it?
Listening?

LEN

I know Jeff can't give you what
you need.

BEV

I don't *need* anything thanks.

BEV holds up her index finger and middle finger.

BEV (CONT'D)

I'm self sufficient.

LEN

I reckon you've forgotten what
it's like to be with a real man.

LEN makes to stroke her breast but she bats his hand away.

BEV

No.

LEN

You think you're too good for me.

BEV

Yes. I do. In fact, I think *all
women* are too good for you. Now
please get out.

LEN

This is *my* house Bev.

BEV

As *I* understand it, it's *Clare's* house. Now go, or I'll start screaming.

LEN

I'd enjoy hearing you scream.

LEN starts trying to kiss and grope her, forcing her back against the dressing table. BEV struggles against his superior size and bulk.

C.U. on the surface of the dressing table. BEV's HAND grabs a pair of hair dressing scissors. BEV plunges the scissors into the top of LEN's bare arm! LEN gasps in pain and releases BEV. He steps back, we see the scissor handles protruding from the top of his arm.

LEN (CONT'D)

You bitch!

LEN steels himself then pulls out the scissors. BEV fixes him with a steely glare.

BEV

'No' means no. So I expect you can guess what 'fuck off' means.

LEN keeps his hand pressed over his wound as he backs towards the door.

LEN

I'm still gonna have you Bev. You fuckin' wait.

LEN gives her a final glare then exits.

SLOW ZOOM INTO C.U. on BEV's face. She exhales in slight relief, but her face is moist eyed and unnerved.

CUT TO:

EXT. - COUNTRY HOUSE - NIGHT

ESTABLISHING SHOT. PULL BACK TO REVEAL the Jacobites ARTHUR and DAVIE standing looking up at the house. DAVIE holds a flaming torch.

C.U. on ARTHUR's face. We see the flicking flames of the torch reflected in the cracked lens of his spectacles.

CUT TO:

INT. - NICHOLLS'S LOUNGE - NIGHT

E.C.U. on a violent video game image on the TV screen. PULL BACK & REVEAL JACK is still playing the game. JEFF is next to the knitting DIANE. MARK smokes a fag in the armchair. NICHOLLS is sorting out some bags of speed from a tupperware container. The ESCORT GIRLS do another line of coke from a 12" album sleeve. The 1st ESCORT GIRL picks up the album and takes it to NICHOLLS, passing him a rolled up tenner.

As he snorts a line, we see the album sleeve is 'Tago Mago' by Can. NICHOLLS offers the sleeve to JEFF. JEFF takes it, does half a line then hesitantly offers it to DIANE. She gives a tiny shake of her head. JEFF offers the sleeve to MARK.

JEFF

Mark?

MARK

Ta.

MARK does a line.

NICHOLLS

You up with Len at the old Fullerton farm then?

JEFF

(nods)

My sister's converted it into a recording studio.

NICHOLLS

One of the oldest buildings 'round here that.

JEFF

How old's this place?

NICHOLLS

This house was built in 1777. On the site of an older house, which was burnt down by the Jacobites in 1745.

MARK

(doubtful)

What were the Jacobites doing all the way over here? This is miles out of their way. They would've been fighting over in Preston.

NICHOLLS

It's true. The main body of men - 'bout four thousand of 'em - were fighting the Battle of Preston.

But Thomas Forster, the Jacobite
leader, also sent a few small
groups of men out further afield.

MARK
Why?

LEADING WITH SOUND we hear a loud crack.

HARD CUT TO:

EXT. - WOODS - NIGHT

E.C.U. on a burning log cracking in a small bonfire. CUT TO REVEAL the bonfire is in a wooded area. MACFISK, ALUN, PATRICK and DOUGLAS are sitting around warming themselves.

NICHOLLS (V.O.)
They were... Terror squads
if you like. Their job was
to spread unrest, unsettle
the community. Poison some
livestock, kick a few heads in,
burn down the odd house.

Another loud crack from the bonfire.

HARD CUT TO:

INT. - NICHOLLS LOUNGE - NIGHT

Everyone is as we left them.

NICHOLLS
There was no rhyme or reason
to any of it. Just random acts
of havoc.

JEFF
Did people die in the fire here?

NICHOLLS
The owners of the house managed to escape. Their housekeeper wasn't so lucky. Burned to death.

HARD CUT TO:

INT. - 18TH CENTURY HOUSE - NIGHT

The hallway to the house is on fire and filling with smoke. An aging HOUSEKEEPER tries to beat back the flames with a witch style broom.

Hard cut to moments later. The HOUSEKEEPER is on fire and screaming and waving the broom around. This is the same image as the vision of the 'witch' the Bikers witnessed in their ritual.

CUT TO:

EXT. - 18TH CENTURY HOUSE - NIGHT

ARTHUR and DAVIE are running away from the burning building.

HARD CUT TO:

INT. - NICHOLLS LOUNGE - NIGHT

C.U. on JEFF's face. We can see he's pondering the connection between what he's been told and the ritual vision.

JEFF
(quietly to himself)
She's not a witch...

MARK
What's that?

JEFF
Um? Nothing.

NICHOLLS holds out a couple of bags of speed. MARK passes him thirty pounds.

NICHOLLS
Stay if you fancy. We're just about to have an orgy.

On the sofa, DIANE gives a barely perceptible head shake.

MARK
(stands up)
Thanks cock, but we got stuff to do.

CUT TO:

EXT. - PENDLE HILL - NIGHT

The car is driving along the country roads. The place seems deserted.

CUT TO:

INT. - BEV'S CAR - NIGHT

JEFF is driving, MARK is in the passenger seat.

MARK
Imagine answering your door like that. Bollock naked.

JEFF
Some people got no self respect.

JEFF's POV: Looking out of the windscreen at the darkened country road illuminated by the headlights. The car rounds a corner and we suddenly see three JACOBITES: DOUGLAS, DAVIE and ARTHUR are standing huddled together talking in the middle of the road.

JEFF (CONT'D)
Jesus!

JEFF slams on the brakes. The car squeals to a halt.

DOUGLAS, DAVIE and ARTHUR remain huddled, facing away from the car, seemingly oblivious, despite being brightly lit by the headlights.

JEFF (CONT'D)
Fuckin' idiots!

MARK
It's okay, I'll have a word.

MARK gets out of the car.

CUT TO:

EXT. - COUNTRY ROAD - CONTINUOUS

MARK walks over to the JACOBITES.

MARK

A'right lads.

DOUGLAS, DAVIE and ARTHUR turn to stare at him, as if noticing the car for the first time.

MARK (CONT'D)

What is it? Historical reenactment society?

DOUGLAS, DAVIE and ARTHUR just stare at him. Or rather through him. There is a weird unearthly energy in the air.

MARK looks at the strangely disengaged faces more closely. Something clicks. MARK understands this is a supernatural occurrence, but he takes it very calmly.

MARK (CONT'D)

Oh right. I get it. Ghosts eh?

As one, DOUGLAS, DAVIE and ARTHUR gently close their eyes. TIGHT ON MARK. He gently closes his eyes.

WIDE JIB SHOT looking down at the white car, and the FOUR FIGURES caught in the headlight beams. A splash of bright light in the blackness of the countryside.

WHITE OUT:

INT. - BEV'S CAR - NIGHT

JEFF is driving, almost as if in a trance. MARK is next to him, smoking. JEFF suddenly comes to his senses and the car jolts to a halt.

MARK
What's up?

JEFF
What, what just happened?

MARK
You slammed the brakes on.

JEFF
No, before that. We, we had to stop because there were... Jacobites blocking the road.

MARK
Historical reenactment society.

JEFF
Was it?

MARK
What else would it be?

JEFF
What did they say to you?

MARK
Nothing. I just told 'em to piss off out the way.

JEFF still looks uncertain. He knows something isn't quite right.

MARK (CONT'D)
So we going back to the studio or what?

A moment's hesitation then JEFF starts the engine.

CUT TO:

INT. - PENDLE HILL - NIGHT

WIDE SHOT of the car driving away down the road. It looks small and vulnerable in the dark night.

HARD CUT TO:

INT. - LIVE ROOM - NIGHT

GRAMS: THE FALL - 'JACOBITES' (00:00).

We watch as MARK and THE FALL play the song. Through the glass we can see CLARE at the desk.

CUT TO:

INT. - SPARE ROOM - NIGHT

GRAMS: (CONTINUE).

BEV is lying in bed. She is deep in thought. JEFF is changing out of his clothes into a T-shirt and pajama bottoms. He climbs into bed and cuddles up to her. BEV gently pushes him away.

GRAMS: (FADE).

BEV

Sorry, my skin's feeling a bit creepy at the moment. Sorry.

JEFF

It's okay. Sorry.

JEFF settles himself down in the bed.

Beat.

BEV
I want to leave here.

JEFF
I know it's not perfect.

BEV
No it's not.

JEFF
We'll only be here another couple of weeks.

BEV
I want to go tomorrow.

JEFF
What's the rush?

BEV
I don't... I don't feel safe here.

JEFF
Why? What's worrying you? Clare really likes you. And I think Len does too.

BEV
I don't want to *discuss* this Jeff. I've made up my mind. I'm going to Gill's in the morning.

JEFF is surprised by the force of her response.

JEFF

Okay, okay.

BEV

I'll stay there until you're finished here, then we'll... We'll work something else out.

JEFF

Erm, okay. Sure.

BEV

I know you said you'd do the painting. That's fine. You stay and finish that. I'll see you when you're done.

JEFF

Okay.

Beat.

BEV switches the light off and the room plunges into darkness.

CUT TO:

EXT. - CLARE'S FARMHOUSE - NIGHT

The farmhouse is illuminated by moonlight.

DISSOLVE TO:

EXT. - WOODS - NIGHT

MACFISK, ALUN, ARTHUR and DAVIE are gathered around a small bonfire, eating some broth. PATRICK and DOUGLAS approach.

ARTHUR
A'right lads?

PATRICK
Aye.

DOUGLAS and PATRICK join them and DOUGLAS helps himself to broth.

ARTHUR
Been busy?

DOUGLAS
Aye.

PATRICK
Blocked a roadway. Killed a field o' sheep.

DOUGLAS
Took a while. They'll nae stay still.

ARTHUR
Did you no use the poison I gave you?

DOUGLAS
Ran oot. Had to break their necks.

MACFISK
(mutters to himself)
Strangling sheep...

PATRICK
(to MacFisk)
What about you two?

MACFISK
Found a farmhouse. Big one.

PATRICK
Did you torch it?

MACFISK and ALUN exchange a glance.

ALUN
No. We er, we---

MACFISK
---The time was nae right. We'll go back.

DAVIE
We burnt down a stable.

ARTHUR
Aye, we did.

DAVIE
And we beat up some youths.

MACFISK
(sarcastic)
Fight the good fight.

PATRICK
(defensive & firm)
Hey, we're all playing our part. This is no rash adventure. This is revolution!

WHITE OUT:

EXT. - CLARE'S FARMHOUSE - MORNING

ESTABLISHING SHOT of the farmhouse bathed in early morning sunlight.

CUT TO:

EXT. - YARD - MORNING

JEFF is helping BEV pack her things into the car boot. JEFF shuts the boot. It springs open again. BEV closes it and it stays closed.

JEFF

Call me when you get there yeah?

BEV

Yeah, course. Hope the painting goes well. Not that it *couldn't* go well. It's not like you're going to use your spade.

They hug. BEV kisses JEFF, but we can see she is more withdrawn than usual.

JEFF

I love you. Don't forget.

BEV

I know. I love you.

BEV hugs him again then gets into the car.

JEFF

Drive safely.

BEV starts the engine. CLARE comes out of the studio and waves. BEV smiles at her. JEFF waves as the car drives off. PULL FOCUS to reveal LEN framed in the kitchen window, watching the car exit the yard.

CUT TO:

INT. - KITCHEN - MORNING

LEN taps his mobile and lifts it to his ear. He has a bandage on his upper arm. He waits for an answer.

LEN

The bitch is tryin' to leave.

CUT TO:

EXT. - YARD - MORNING

CLARE gives JEFF a hug.

Beat.

CLARE

You okay?

JEFF

Yeah. Yeah, I'm... Yeah. Thanks.

CLARE

Everything alright with Bev? You and her still...?

JEFF

Yeah.

Beat.

JEFF (CONT'D)
Still what?

CLARE
Solid?

JEFF
Solid? Yeah. Yeah we're solid.

CLARE
I thought so. She's lovely. You
don't want to lose her.

JEFF
(smiles)
I'm not going to lose her.
Don't worry.

Beat.

JEFF (CONT'D)
What about you and Len? Solid?

Beat.

CLARE
(nods)
Ish.

CLARE glances towards the house to check Len isn't looking or within earshot. CLARE and JEFF exchange a smirk. They walk away from the house toward the studio. They still speak in hushed tones.

JEFF
Ish? You can't be solid-*ish*.
There's no such thing. You're
either solid or you're... unstable.

CLARE hesitates before saying more.

CLARE

Do you, do you think Len's weird?

JEFF is uncertain how honest to be.

JEFF

Is he weird? Erm, well, I think you could say there was something weird about him.

CLARE

That's the same thing. Look, I want you to be honest with me. Say what you think.

JEFF

Okay. Well, in that case, what I'm thinking is 'what the hell do you see in him!?'

CLARE

(sighs)

He was fun at first. We used to have a good laugh, do stuff together...

JEFF

And now?

CLARE

(sighs)

I dunno. The spark seems to have gone. To be honest, since he joined that gang, it's like he's put everything else on hold.

Across the yard, the farmhouse door opens and LEN steps out. JEFF and CLARE can't help but guiltily glance over. LEN smiles at them as he crosses the yard and heads toward the garage.

CLARE (CONT'D)
I should get everything set up for the group.

JEFF
(nods)
Yeah. I best get this painting started.

CLARE enters the studio and JEFF makes his way across the yard to the house.

CUT TO:

EXT. - FIELD - MORNING

C.U. on a COW lying on grass. At first we assume it is asleep.

CUT TO WIDE SHOT: The whole herd of COWS are lying dead in the field. We hear a car engine.

CUT TO:

EXT. - COUNTRY ROAD - MORNING

Bev's car drives down the quiet roads. She's pretty much the only car on the road.

CUT TO:

INT. - BEV'S CAR - MORNING

BEV is at the wheel. Her spirits seem to have lifted a little. Suddenly, she hears the multiple roar of motorbike engines approaching. She looks in the rearview mirror.

CUT TO:

EXT. - COUNTRY ROAD - MORNING

FOUR BIKERS on loud motorbikes come roaring up close behind the car, loud and menacing like big black flies. They wear black leathers and their helmets with reflective visors.

CUT TO:

INT. - BEV'S CAR - MORNING

BEV is clearly unnerved. She tries to accelerate away.

CUT TO:

EXT. - COUNTRY ROAD - MORNING

The BIKERS easily keep pace with the car. Two of them pull up alongside the car, menacingly close, trying to force her off the road.

CUT TO:

INT. - BEV'S CAR - MORNING

Determined not to be out-maneuvered, BEV gives the steering wheel a slight jerk to one side.

CUT TO:

EXT. - COUNTRY ROAD - MORNING

The car nudges against one of the BIKERS, causing his bike to wobble and go veering off. The bike hits a dry stone wall and the BIKER goes flying over the handlebars.

The three remaining speeding BIKERS close in on Bev's car.

CUT TO:

INT. - BEV'S CAR - MORNING

BEV is starting to panic. The BIKER's silver visored helmet stares in through the passenger window, with evil intent. BEV looks back at the road ahead.

BEV's POV: There's a CYCLIST just ahead. She automatically swerves to avoid him. In doing so, BEV loses control of the car.

CUT TO:

EXT. - COUNTRY ROAD - MORNING

Bev's car goes spinning out of control and collides with the wall.

CUT TO:

INT. - BEV'S CAR - MORNING

At the point of collision, the airbag goes off. BEV is dazed but seems physically okay. Her breathing is laboured, she pulls out her inhaler and takes a hit. Then another.

She has a moment where her breathing calms, then suddenly her door is pulled open. A helmeted BIKER reaches in, unfastens her seat belt and pulls her roughly from the car.

CUT TO:

EXT. - ROADSIDE - CONTINUOUS

BEV is dragged from the car by the FIRST BIKER. He pushes BEV roughly towards the other two BIKERS. They grab her. BEV is very dazed. The FIRST BIKER approaches her. The CYCLIST rides up and dismounts. He's appalled by their behaviour.

CYCLIST

What the hell are you doing!?

Suddenly the FIRST BIKER pulls out a Stanley knife and swiftly slashes it across both of the CYCLIST's wrists.

CYCLIST (CONT'D)

Shit! Shit! Shit!

The CYCLIST wanders around in a helpless panic as blood sprays from both his wrists.

CYCLIST (CONT'D)

You bastards! Shit! Shit!

Suddenly the INJURED BIKER who was knocked off his bike comes limping up. He still wears his helmet but the silver visor is crazed.

BEV's POV: The INJURED BIKER is staring at her with his crazed visor. Behind him, the CYCLIST is staggering around as he loses more and more blood.

Suddenly he collapses out of shot. A moment later and the INJURED BIKER throws a punch towards BEV and we...

CUT TO BLACK:

INT. - LIVE ROOM - DAY

GRAMS: THE FALL - 'UNTITLED' (00:00).

MARK and THE FALL are playing a song.

CUT TO:

INT. - STUDIO CONTROL ROOM - DAY

GRAMS: (CONTINUE).

CLARE is at the mixing desk. She takes the empty reel box and takes a pen to write on it. But for some reason the pen won't make a mark. She shakes the pen and tries again. She chucks the pen in the bin and takes another from a mug of pens and pencils. She tries that. Nothing. She tries a pencil. But nothing seems to make a mark. Eventually CLARE finds a sharpie and writes *'The Fall'* on the box.

CUT TO:

EXT. - WOODS - DAY

GRAMS: (CONTINUE).

MACFISK and ALUN are walking through the woods. They pass an old wooden signpost marked *'Well Spring'* with an arrow pointing in the direction they are walking.

GRAMS: (FADE).

ALUN

You're quiet.

MACFISK

I've had enough. I think we should go.

ALUN

Go home?

MACFISK

No. To battle.

ALUN

(uncertain)

Eh? What, now?

MACFISK

Aye. We've travelled half way down the country. And for *what?* To do *what?* To end up no better than playing pranks.

ALUN

Shhhh...

ALUN gestures for MACFISK to be quiet and listen. They hear the sound of an acoustic guitar gently playing.

MACFISK and ALUN carefully make their way in between the trees as they follow the sound of music.

CUT TO:

EXT. - WELL SPRING - DAY

GRAMS: 'LO! THE BIRD HAS FALLEN' (00:00).

MARY is sitting on a tree stump, eyes closed, gently playing her acoustic guitar.

MACFISK and ALUN step out from the trees and walk toward her.

The well spring begins to bubble, making strange sounds. MACFISK and ALUN stare at it intrigued.

F/X SHOT: A strange foam starts bubbling up in the well. It glows with an odd yellow light and it pours out in serpent like coils. There is something very strange, magical and unsettling happening.

ALUN

What is it?

MACFISK

Magic...

ALUN reaches out towards the coils of foam.

F/X SHOT: His fingers touch the foam and it quickly coils and bubbles around his hand.

ALUN

(gasps)

It's ice cold.

ALUN pulls his hand away.

F/X SHOT: The foam solidifies into a strange thick yellow/grey mucus-like growth covering his hand. ALUN slumps down to the ground. MACFISK makes to help him, but ALUN pushes him away. ALUN curls into a fetal position nursing the strange growth on the back of his hand. MACFISK staggers back then runs off in fear.

Eyes closed in a trance-like state, MARY continues to play and begins to sing.

MARY (V.O.)
(sings)
Spying this Jacobite,
Atop a roof far distant...

DISSOLVE TO:

INT. - ABANDONED BARN - DAY

GRAMS: (CONTINUE.)

BEV's POV: She has some sacking over her head. Hints of daylight through the weave. We hear BEV's worried breathing.

Suddenly, the cloth is pulled off revealing the INJURED BIKER looking down at us with his crazed silver visor.

MARY (V.O.)
(sings)
Edward called a musket man,
To serve as his assistant...

CUT TO WIDE SHOT: BEV is tied to an old chair in the middle of the barn. She's bruised, dishevelled and the INJURED BIKER stands menacingly before her.

CUT TO:

INT. - CLARE'S BACK ROOM - DAY

GRAMS: (CONT.)

JEFF wears a scruffy paint splattered T-shirt about a quarter of a way through painting the walls. The furniture has been gathered together in the centre of the room and covered with old bed sheets.

MARY (V.O.)
(sings)
Two salvoes true and mighty,
Rang from the sportsman's gun...

JEFF puts down his paint brush, sips from a mug of tea and takes out his mobile.

C.U. on the mobile in his hand. We see him select Bev's number and call her. He lifts the mobile to his ear. It rings and rings.

DISSOLVE TO:

INT. - ABANDONED BARN - DAY

BEV's mobile is ringing. She's tied to the chair and unable to answer it.

The INJURED BIKER reaches into BEV's jeans pocket and pulls out her mobile. As he does so, we see her inhaler fall out and tumble onto the ground.

BEV
Hey, that's mine.

The INJURED BIKER looks at the mobile then drops it on the ground and stamps on it. The mobile shatters and stops ringing.

The barn doors open and another BIKER steps inside. He takes off his helmet. It's LEN. He gives BEV a humourless smile, then walks over to her. BEV is infuriated and repulsed by him.

LEN
Bev... Good to see you.

BEV
Here he is: Mr Cunt.

LEN
Insulting your captor.
Is that wise?

Beat.

BEV
You went to all this trouble, because I wouldn't let you grope me?

LEN
This was no trouble at all. The trouble hasn't started yet.

LEN smiles at her. BEV still looks focussed, but we can tell she's scared.

CUT TO:

INT. - STUDIO CONTROL ROOM - DAY

C.U. on a tape box upon which is scrawled '*THE FALL EP - Master 1*'. Underneath there is a song title and some notes.

CLARE is fiddling with a reel to reel tape. A concerned JEFF enters the control room.

CLARE

Hiya. Mark's coming in a bit. We're gonna start mixing.

JEFF

Great.

JEFF stands awkwardly, unsure whether or not to speak.

JEFF (CONT'D)

I'm, I'm a bit worried about Bev.

CLARE

Why?

JEFF

She's not answering her mobile.

CLARE

Maybe her battery died.

JEFF

I phoned Gill. Bev hasn't arrived. She *should* have been there two hours ago.

CLARE ponders this for a moment. She hesitates then speaks.

CLARE

You don't think...

JEFF

What?

CLARE

You don't think Bev's... dumped you without telling you?

JEFF

What? No.

CLARE

Or that maybe she's hiding something from you?

JEFF

Like what?

CLARE

Like an affair?

JEFF

I don't think so. No...

JEFF drifts into uncertain thought.

JEFF (CONT'D)

Oh I don't know. Maybe. Maybe she *has* dumped me without telling me. I was gonna phone the police. I'm not sure now. Don't wanna look like a dick.

CUT TO:

INT. - ABANDONED BARN - DAY

LEN is standing looking down at BEV tied to the chair.

LEN

I love how quiet it is in the country.

BEV
So what's the plan? Rape me? Rape me then kill me?

Beat.

BEV (CONT'D)
Then get caught and sent down?

LEN begins to walk slowly in a circle around BEV.

LEN
D'yer wanna know the really exciting thing Bev?

LEN looks at her expectantly. She doesn't respond.

LEN (CONT'D)
There *is* no plan.

LEN walks behind BEV, out of her view.

LEN (CONT'D)
There *is* no plan.

C.U. on BEV's tense face. LEN is somewhere out of view behind her.

LEN (O.S.) (CONT'D)
Anything could happen.

BEV slowly closes her eyes in fear.

Beat.

LEN (CONT'D)
Any fucking thing.

CUT TO:

EXT. - HILLSIDE - DAY

WIDE SHOT overlooking the Barn. PULL BACK to reveal MACFISK is standing, staring uncertainly at the building.

MACFISK's expression is fearful and exhausted. He hears an approaching car engine. He turns to see Ed's car driving along the nearby road.

CUT TO:

INT. - ED'S CAR - DAY

ED is in the driving seat. MARK is next to him and PETER in the back. PETER winces and mutters to himself.

PETER

Fuck.

ED

What?

PETER

Tooth ache. Suddenly come on. Wonder if they've got any pain killers at the studio.

MARK

I was told at school in '72 that science would erase pain and disease by 2010. But, when I had shingles last year, I was in constant pain 20 hours a day. Coz the orthodox doctor won't give codeine pain killers to drinkers.

PETER
What did he give you?

MARK
He offered me fucking paracetamol, false drugs and anti-depressants!

ED
That's no fucking use.

MARK
Exactly. They're for bed wetters. I've never took anti-depressants. And I don't intend to pollute my body balance of pure street drugs, water and spirits.

PETER and ED chuckle.

CUT TO:

INT. - ABANDONED BARN - DAY

BEV is tied to the chair and LEN is standing right behind her. BEV is nervous and her breathing is a little uneven. LEN leans over and kisses the top of BEV's head. BEV jolts her head away.

Beat.

LEN
So jumpy Bev. Good thing you're strapped down.

LEN grabs BEV's hair and kisses her cheek. She struggles but LEN holds her firmly. He licks her cheek and she starts to breathe heavily and unevenly.

LEN (CONT'D)
That's it. Yer getting into it now. Bit of heavy breathing.

BEV
It's an asthma attack you pillock!

BEV (CONT'D)
(nods to the floor)
My inhaler's down there.

LEN stares down at the inhaler on the ground.

LEN
Ah.

LEN picks it up, tosses it and catches it.

LEN (CONT'D)
You in the mood then are you?

BEV's breathing is becoming heavier and more croaky. LEN steps up to her, holding the inhaler just inches away from her face and slowly moving it around in a teasing manner.

LEN (CONT'D)
In the mood for a blast on the old orgasmatron?

BEV is starting to cough. LEN flicks the cover off the end of the inhaler.

LEN (CONT'D)
Open wide.

BEV opens her mouth but LEN merely traces around the edge of her lips with the end of the inhaler.

BEV

Come on!

LEN puts the end of the inhaler in her mouth.

LEN

Are you ready to suck it for me?

The bleary eyed BEV just stares up at him.

LEN (CONT'D)

And...

He makes to depress the inhaler and BEV breaths in. But at the last minute LEN pulls it away, spraying it into the air.

LEN (CONT'D)

Oh dear...

BEV continues to gasp for breath as she stares up at LEN with anger in her eyes. LEN grabs BEV's chin and sticks the end of the inhaler in her mouth.

LEN (CONT'D)

And... suck.

LEN depresses the inhaler and BEV breaths in.

LEN (CONT'D)

Good girl.

BEV's breathing still isn't quite settled.

LEN (CONT'D)
Sounds like you might be in need of multiple orgasms.

BEV opens her mouth. LEN inserts the inhaler and depresses it again. BEV inhales and her breathing gradually settles.

LEN (CONT'D)
There.

LEN strokes BEV's cheek and she flinches slightly.

CUT TO:

INT. - STUDIO CONTROL ROOM - DAY

JEFF is talking into his mobile. CLARE is tidying up, picking up bits of trash and putting them in a carrier bag.

JEFF
Okay. Yeah, no, I understand what you're saying. Okay. Okay, thanks. Bye.

JEFF switches off his mobile.

Beat.

JEFF (CONT'D)
Right, I've given all Bev's details to the police. They've got my number. But to be honest the woman didn't sound that interested.

CLARE

Oh well, at least you've tried.
I mean what else can you do?

JEFF

You think she's dumped me
don't you.

CLARE

No. I don't. I just mentioned
that as an option. There's plenty
of other possibilities.

JEFF

Go on then...

CLARE

She's gone off somewhere on her
own to get her head together.
She's... gone to her Mum's?

JEFF

Rung her Mum. She's not there.

CLARE

Then maybe she's... I don't know.

JEFF

You're *convinced* she's dumped me.

CLARE

I'm not! Anyway what do you
prefer, she's dumped you, or
she's lying dead somewhere!?

JEFF

What!? Am I supposed to choose!?

CLARE

(back-peddling)

No. Sorry. I shouldn't have said that. No, no, I'm just saying, Bev having dumped you isn't the worst possible outcome.

JEFF

(sarcastic)

Cooool. Well, thanks for that.

CLARE

I'm sorry.

JEFF shakes his head and exits. CLARE is about to follow him then decides to give him some space.

CUT TO:

EXT. - YARD - DAY

The disgruntled JEFF exits the studio and wanders across the yard to the farmhouse.

As he opens the door and steps inside, Ed's car drives up into the yard and parks. MARK and PETER climb out.

ED

Ring us when yer ready to be picked up yeah.

PETER

We'll be a few hours I reckon.

MARK

Cheers cock.

ED reverses the car out of the yard. MARK and PETER walk towards the studio.

CUT TO:

INT. - KITCHEN - DAY

JEFF is making himself a coffee. He's deep in thought. He pours hot water into a mug, stirs in milk, picks it up and turns around. Suddenly he's face to face with the silver visored helmet of a crash helmeted BIKER! JEFF gives a start, accidentally spilling hot coffee on himself. The BIKER's gloved hands remove the helmet to reveal LEN.

JEFF

Shit Len. Made me jump. When did you get back? Didn't hear your bike.

LEN

I know you didn't. Coz I parked up quarter of a mile back. Didn't want Clare to know I was here.

JEFF

Why?

LEN

Sons of Witches business. I need you to come with me.

JEFF

Eh?

LEN

It's something special.

JEFF
What, right now?

LEN
Yeah. Come on.

JEFF
No, I can't. Not now.

LEN
(stern)
You don't have a choice.

JEFF
What d'yer m---

LEN grabs him roughly.

LEN
This isn't a pissin' pick and mix thing pal. You're a Son of a Witch. You've been called. You come. End of.

JEFF
Bev's gone missing.

LEN
What?

LEN's mood softens considerably and he releases JEFF.

LEN (CONT'D)
Really?

JEFF
She's just disappeared. I phoned the police but...

LEN
Fucking useless?

JEFF nods.

LEN (CONT'D)
Worrying innit. Are you worried?

JEFF
Course I am.

Beat.

LEN
Sons of Witches'll sort it.

JEFF
What? How?

LEN
If she's still in the area we can find her. There's enough of us. We know Pendle like the back of our hands, we can check all the pubs. Check if her car's been abandoned anywhere.

JEFF
Brilliant. Good idea.

LEN
Course if she's gone further afield... Do you think she might have dumped you?

JEFF
She's not fucking dumped me!

LEN

Come on.

LEN moves off. JEFF makes to follow him.

LEN (CONT'D)

We'll go do this ritual, then we'll find Bev.

JEFF stops in his tracks.

JEFF

Ritual?

LEN turns and nods.

LEN

That's why I come to fetch you. We're doing a ritual. We're chaos magicians. We all need to be there.

JEFF

I don't want to see the witch again. I'm stressed out as it is.

LEN

All I can tell you is, if you don't come now, the others will come and they'll find you and they'll fuck you up.

(shrugs)

So come now and everybody's still smiling.

JEFF looks at him and gives a sigh.

CUT TO:

INT. - STUDIO CONTROL ROOM - DAY

MARK and PETER are sitting on the sofa. MARK sifts through a wad of hand written notes. PETER is talking on his mobile.

PETER
Okay. I'll see you at ten thirty. Bye.

PETER switches off his mobile.

PETER (CONT'D)
Got an appointment in the morning.

Enter CLARE with a large glass of water with two soluble painkillers dissolving in it. She passes it to PETER.

CLARE
That should take the edge off.

PETER
Thanks.

CLARE
(joking)
Mark, can I get you one?

MARK
No I'm good ta.

CLARE takes a stack of tape boxes off the shelf - all marked '*The Fall*' - and puts them down by the reel to reel.

CLARE
Which track d'yer wanna start with?

MARK
Whatever order they come up.

A series of swift C.U.s: CLARE's HANDS taking the spool from the box, placing it on the reel to reel, threading the tape through the heads onto the empty reel.

C.U. on CLARE's FINGER pressing the 'Play' button.

C.U. on the tape running through the head. A second later, we hear the sound of an acoustic guitar and we hear old Mary singing 'Lo! The Bird is Fallen'.

GRAMS: 'LO! THE BIRD HAS FALLEN'.

MARY (V.O.)
(sings)
And lo! "The bird is fallen",
Raised cheers from everyone...

PETER
(laughs)
Not what I was expecting.

CLARE
Oops not that one. Somebody's put this in the wrong box.

CLARE switches off the tape, rewinds it and removes the reel. She puts it on top of the box. It clearly says '*The Fall*' on the box.

CLARE (CONT'D)
Sorry. Here we go.

CLARE removes another tape box marked 'The Fall' from a shelf, takes out the reel, threads it on the player and presses play. We hear the click of drum sticks counting in then the band starts up.

GRAMS: TRACK ONE by THE FALL.

After 25 seconds or so, there's a sudden weird crackling on the tape and the sound of the band is replaced by the sound of Mary singing again.

GRAMS: 'LO! THE BIRD HAS FALLEN'.

MARY (V.O.)
(sings)
And so it was that famous day,
That Edward was called brave...

CLARE looks confused. MARK looks displeased.

CLARE
This is weird.

MARK
What's going on?

CLARE
I'm... not sure.

CLARE stops the tape, presses 'fast forward' then 'stop' then 'play'. Again Mary's singing comes from the speakers.

MARY (V.O.)
(sings)
For many a loyal soldier's life,
His gallantry did save.

C.U. on CLARE's puzzled face.

CUT TO:

EXT. - ABANDONED BARN - DAY

There are four motorbikes parked up outside. LEN drives up on his bike with JEFF riding pillion. LEN cuts the engine and they dismount. LEN takes out his mobile and checks it.

LEN

Can I see your mobile?

JEFF hands over his mobile. LEN immediately flings the mobile over the high wall and out of sight in the field beyond.

JEFF

What!?

LEN

It's important. Come on.

LEN grabs JEFF's arm and leads him into the barn.

CUT TO:

INT. - ABANDONED BARN - DAY

The barn door opens and LEN enters holding JEFF by the arm. JEFF is surprised to see the barn is empty. A shaft of light shines down through a large hole in the roof, illuminating a patch of ground.

JEFF

Where's everybody else?

LEN
Don't fuss.

JEFF
When you say ritual...

LEN
Jeff. Don't fuss.

JEFF
(sarcastic)
Don't fuss? Sorry I don't know the etiquette for bike gang rituals!

LEN's heavy gloved hand grabs JEFF by the throat.

LEN
(hisses)
This is a sacred time. So shut yer fuckin' cake hole!

LEN relaxes his grip on JEFF. JEFF rubs his neck. They hear a creak from across the barn. They both turn to look.

JEFF's POV: At first we cannot penetrate the darkness of the far side of the barn. Then five figures appear out of the darkness and walk slowly toward the shaft of sunlight. There are FOUR BIKERS in leathers and silver visored black helmets.

Between them they are leading a fifth figure. It's a VEILED WOMAN. She wears a black cloak covering her body and a thick black veil concealing her face. It is her slender neck and bare legs and feet which tell us the figure is female.

JEFF looks up. His initial reaction is shock. He speaks to LEN in a hushed tone.

JEFF
What's going on?
(to Len)
Please tell me you're not gonna kill her?

LEN
Course not. It's a sex ritual.

C.U. on JEFF's concerned face.

CUT TO:

INT. - STUDIO CONTROL ROOM - DAY

C.U. on the tape spool rewinding. CUT TO REVEAL a worried looking CLARE standing examining a couple of tape boxes labelled *'The Fall'*.

MARK
So, let's get this straight. Have you recorded over our track?

CLARE
No. No, definitely not.

MARK
Well that's what it fucking sounds like.

Doubt descends on CLARE's face.

CLARE
No, that couldn't have happened. I recorded Mary *before* you arrived.

CLARE stops the tape and presses fast forward then stop then play. Again Mary's singing comes from the speakers.

GRAMS: 'LO! THE BIRD HAS FALLEN'.

MARY (V.O.)
(sings)
In honour of this noble deed...

CLARE
Shit!

CLARE switches off the tape, rewinds it and removes the reel. MARK and PETER exchange a look.

MARK
Unbelievable.

CLARE
All I can think, is somebody has come in here and deliberately done it as a prank. And when I find out who...

MARK
(sarcastic)
Yeah, let me know when you find out.

CLARE takes another tape box off the shelf. This one is also marked *'The Fall'*. CLARE threads the reel on the player and presses play. After a second, we hear Mark's voice intoning, close mic'd and.

GRAMS: TRACK THREE by THE FALL.

MARK (V.O.)
Its truth was amazing. O Joy!
Solaris-like!

CUT TO:

INT. - ABANDONED BARN - DAY

GRAMS: (CONTINUE).

The VEILED WOMAN is standing in the shaft of moonlight. The FOUR BIKERS stand around her facing outward. JEFF and LEN stand a few feet away, looking on.

MARK (V.O.)
White and translucent foams.

The VEILED WOMAN drops her cloak. She is completely naked.

MARK (V.O.)
It squirmed unfettered, energised
in wondrous coil.

JEFF is embarrassed by her nakedness and turns away from her.

At that moment the sound of the band kicks in.

CUT BACK TO:

INT. - STUDIO CONTROL ROOM - DAY

GRAMS: (CONTINUE).

MARK, CLARE and PETER are listening to the recording. Suddenly there's more crackling on the tape and the sound of Mary singing cuts in replacing The Fall.

GRAMS: 'LO! THE BIRD HAS FALLEN'.

MARY (V.O.)
(sings)
His name through all the country...

MARK
What the fuck's going on? This is quite disrespectful actually.

CLARE
(confused and worried)
This can't be right.

MARK
No, it *isn't* right.

CLARE
It's not possible.

CLARE stops and rewinds the tape. We hear Mary's singing and guitar playing at high speed in reverse. The spools run to an end and CLARE turns to MARK. She's shaken and very apologetic.

CLARE (CONT'D)
Mark, I am *so* sorry. We've never had a problem anything like this before. I can't understand what's happened.

MARK
What's happened love, is you have wasted The Fall's time. We've

been coming here for a fucking
week and wasting our time!

CUT TO:

INT. - ABANDONED BARN - DAY

JEFF stands staring at the VEILED WOMAN and the BIKERS. The BIKER with a crazed visor pulls the cloak from the VEILED WOMAN revealing her nakedness. JEFF turns away in embarrassment and speaks quietly to LEN.

JEFF
I'm not... the sex ritual type.
What are we supposed to be doing?

LEN
(nods to the bikers)
Each of us is gonna fuck her.
Then you're gonna fuck her.

JEFF pulls a face.

JEFF
(pulls a face)
Ur. No, sorry this isn't me.

LEN
It is. You're a Son of a Witch.

JEFF
Who is she anyway?

LEN
A cleaner.

JEFF

A cleaner?

LEN

A cleaner. She's up for it.

JEFF turns back to glance at the VEILED WOMAN and a look of recognition settles on his face.

JEFF

That's Bev!

LEN

No it isn't.

JEFF

It bloody is! I've been with her for five years. I know what her body looks like!

JEFF marches over and pulls the veil off the WOMAN's head.

F/X SHOT: C.U. on the veil as it is pulled away revealing not Bev, but the burning WITCH! She hovers a foot above the ground, holding her broom, burning and silently screaming!

JEFF recoils in fear.

HARD CUT TO:

INT. - DARKENED CONFINED SPACE - NIGHT

E.C.U. on BEV's unconscious face. She has been gagged with a biker's handkerchief. After a split second, she blinks into sudden, wide-eyed consciousness. It is very dark, but BEV spots something close by and squirms in horror.

CUT TO REVEAL she is tied up in the fetal position in the confined space. Her body is in fact resting on top of the corpse of the murdered, blood stained CYCLIST.

C.U. on his dead face, his eyes soulless, his slack mouth hanging open.

The gagged and helpless BEV is on the verge of panic.

HARD CUT TO:

INT. - ABANDONED BARN - NIGHT

JEFF is frightened of the hovering, flaming WITCH, but unable to move.

F/X SHOT: Suddenly, the flames which cover the WITCH are reduced to a gentle flicker. There is a sudden quiet in the air.

F/X SHOT: JEFF glances around to see that it is as if he and the WITCH are in an area of glistening light separated from LEN and the BIKERS. The WITCH speaks in a broad but croaky Lancastrian accent.

WITCH

You were expecting to see your lover?

JEFF takes a moment to recover his nerve before he can reply.

JEFF

Yes. Bev. Do you know where she is?

WITCH

They have her close by.
She's alive.

JEFF

Thank God.

WITCH

You're different to them.

JEFF

Yeah I am.

WITCH

Your being here has changed everything.

JEFF

Has it?

WITCH

These men have stalked this land too long. They are already doomed. But you are not. You should go.

JEFF

I'd... I'd like that.

WITCH

Be gone.

Suddenly the flames flare up again and the area of light around them disappears. Gathering himself together, JEFF runs away from the WITCH and through the circle of BIKERS. A second later and LEN seems to come to his senses. He turns and runs after JEFF.

LEN catches up with JEFF just as JEFF reaches the barn doors. JEFF swiftly pulls the door back towards LEN slamming it directly in LEN's face.

We see the edge of the door contact with LEN's face, sending him reeling backwards.
JEFF goes running out of the barn.

A second later, LEN gets to his feet and darts after him.

CUT TO:

EXT. - ABANDONED BARN - CONTINUOUS

LEN darts out of the barn, glances about and sees that all the motorbikes are still there. He searches around for JEFF.

HARD CUT TO:

INT. - STUDIO CONTROL ROOM - DAY

CLARE is still trying to patch things up with the angry MARK.

MARK
I'm angry for the group as well.
The group have been working
fucking hard actually!

CLARE
I know. I know. This is dreadful.

PETER takes another Fall reel box off the shelf.

PETER
What about this one?

Whilst they are talking, PETER is threading up the next Fall spool on the tape player.

CLARE

Only me and Len have got keys, so I don't see how... Len wouldn't...

MARK

Well *somebody* has.

CLARE

Look, let me make it up to you. You can have three weeks free studio time here.

MARK

I don't *want* to spend any more time here. It's not acceptable. It's not fit for purpose.

PETER presses play.

GRAMS: THE FALL - 'JACOBITES' (00.00).

A loud rock track throbs from the speakers. They listen for 15 seconds or so. CLARE bites her bottom lip in anticipation.

MARK (CONT'D)

(sarcastic)

So when's the old woman gonna come in then?

CLARE is nervously waiting to see if the track is going to be interrupted. However, the track continues. Mark's vocal starts up, then suddenly there's a crackle and the recording of Mary comes in.

GRAMS: 'LO! THE BIRD HAS FALLEN'.

CLARE

Shit!

CUT TO:

EXT. - ABANDONED BARN - DAY

LEN is searching the yard for JEFF. He passes a tractor. Suddenly JEFF looms up behind one of the large tractor tires and loops an oily metal bike chain around LEN's neck! JEFF tugs him backwards, slamming the biker's body back against the tire.

LEN gasps for air! He claws at the chain around his throat! He tries to reach around and grab at JEFF. But JEFF's body is protected on the other side of the large tire.

JEFF

(hissing in Len's ear)

Where's Bev?

LEN gurgles incomprehensibly. JEFF loosens the chain ever so slightly.

JEFF (CONT'D)

Say again.

LEN

I can show you.

JEFF tightens the chain again.

JEFF

No! You can tell me!

JEFF relaxes the chain slightly. LEN coughs and catches his breath.

JEFF (CONT'D)

Well?

LEN

Round the back of the barn...

LEN gestures vaguely with his hand.

JEFF

Where?

LEN gasps and goes limp. JEFF releases the chain. LEN collapses. JEFF looks down at LEN's body, shocked at what he's done. After a moment's hesitation he walks forwards.

Suddenly LEN's hand grabs JEFF's ankle. JEFF almost stumbles, then turns and viciously whacks LEN's head with the bike chain a couple of times. We hear the awful sound of metal against skin and bone.

The bloody LEN slumps against the tarmac. The shell-shocked JEFF drops the chain and moves swiftly away.

JEFF rushes past the barn doors. The doors are slightly ajar, the strange flickering light coming from inside.

CUT TO:

INT. - ABANDONED BARN - DAY

The FOUR BIKERS still stand around the burning WITCH.

WITCH
I know you. I know you well.

The BIKERS remove their helmets. When we see their faces, we recognise them as the faces of the JACOBITES! PATRICK, DOUGLAS and DAVIE.

Finally, the INJURED BIKER with the crazed visor removes his helmet to reveal ARTHUR with his cracked spectacle lens.

HARD CUT TO:

EXT. - ABANDONED BARN - DAY

JEFF rounds the corner and sees Bev's empty car parked up next to a high wall. The corner of the bonnet is smashed in from the crash earlier. JEFF glances around then becomes aware of a very muffled moaning. He sees the car is rocking slightly.

JEFF goes to the car and fiddles with the boot lock. Eventually it pops open to reveal the distraught BEV coiled up with the CYCLIST'S CORPSE. BEV's eyes are wide with relief.

JEFF
Oh thank God.

JEFF helps BEV out of the boot. He unties the handkerchief gagging her mouth. And the rope from her wrists.

BEV

Oh fuck. I thought...
I thought...

They hug. Suddenly JEFF notices the CYCLIST'S CORPSE in the boot next to the spade. JEFF stares down at the body.

JEFF

Who is he?

BEV

Somebody who tried to help.

JEFF hesitantly bends down to look at the CYCLIST'S CORPSE.

JEFF

Poor bugger.

BEV

(tearful)

Jeff, I can't stay here.

TIGHT SHOT on JEFF as he stands up straight.

JEFF

Course. Let's go. My mobile's somewhere over that wall.

Suddenly, a bike chain whacks JEFF around the head! JEFF cries out in agony, clutches at his face and crumples to his knees.

CUT TO REVEAL LEN standing over him. LEN's face is cut, gory and bruised from the earlier chain attack. LEN whacks him with the chain again, this time hitting JEFF on the shoulder.

JEFF falls sideways gasping in pain. LEN stands over him.

LEN

You fuckin' bastard!

LEN lifts the bike chain aloft!

C.U. on JEFF as he covers his face! Off screen, we hear a grunt and a quick cutting thudding sound. A second later, JEFF uncovers his eyes. He is shocked by what he sees.

CUT TO REVEAL: BEV has plunged the spade through the front of LEN's head! The blade has penetrated his face just below the eyes and has sunk a good four and half inches into his face. Yet still he stands, with the spade sticking out horizontally.

The injured JEFF scrabbles to his feet. He and BEV stagger away from LEN. But the facially impaled LEN staggers after them, groaning in anger and agony! The shovel still sticking out horizontally from his face like a long Dalek eye stalk!

HARD CUT TO:

INT. - ABANDONED BARN - DAY

The burning WITCH is still hovering a foot above the ground, surrounded by PATRICK, DOUGLAS, DAVIE and ARTHUR in the Biker's leathers.

WITCH

Your cause was noble. But your deeds were terrible.

PATRICK, DOUGLAS, DAVIE and ARTHUR look awkwardly down at the ground.

WITCH (CONT'D)
The battle is lost. The campaign is lost. It was lost long ago. You shouldn't still be here. None of us should!

HARD CUT TO:

EXT. - HILLSIDE - DAY

E.C.U. on MACFISK's contorted face. He's flat on his back with his hands over his ears and is having some sort of fit. He twitches and spasms, gasping for air.

HARD CUT TO:

INT. - STUDIO CONTROL ROOM - DAY

GRAMS: 'LO! THE BIRD HAS FALLEN'.

PETER
(sighs loudly)
So every single one of our recordings has been sabotaged.

CLARE nods silently. MARK grabs his jacket and puts it on.

MARK
Right we're going.
(to Peter)
Phone Ed, get him to pick us up.

PETER takes out his mobile and taps at it.

CLARE
Honestly Mark, I will make things alright.

MARK
It's too late for that! Coz you or one of your fucking sheep shagging family has recorded all over our stuff with that daft old woman.

MARK heads out of the room. PETER follows. A second later we hear the front door open and slam.

C.U. on CLARE's face, her expression a mix of frustration and anger.

CUT TO:

EXT. - ABANDONED BARN - DAY

BEV and JEFF are trapped in the corner of the barn yard. On one side, a high brick wall, on the other, a large metal feed container.

LEN stands before them, terrifying in his groaning anger and agony! The shovel still sticks out from his face, the handle swinging from one side to the other as he turns his head. JEFF and BEV have to avoid being hit by it. He tries to pull it out, but there is too much blood on the shaft and it's too slippery.

JEFF makes a dive to one side. LEN turns his head swiftly and by sheer fluke, the hard handle of the spade ends up thwacking JEFF in the temple. JEFF is knocked off balance! He staggers sideways, bangs his head into the metal container and falls dazed to the floor.

LEN turns back to BEV. She stumbles away from him, trips and falls over backwards onto the ground. BEV is helpless!

LEN stands over her, arms outstretched, roaring threateningly, the spade handle protruding from his face. BEV is terrified. She screams! Suddenly LEN stiffens and falls towards her!

BEV rolls away to one side and safety.

LEN falls forwards, the handle of the spade hits the tarmac with a hard thud. The force of this causes the blade of the spade to pass through the rest of LEN's face, slicing off the top of his head!

C.U. on the top of LEN's head as it rolls around and around on the tarmac before coming to rest.

The shocked and bruised JEFF and BEV crawl across the ground towards each other.

CUT TO:

EXT. - WELL SPRING - DAY

GRAMS: 'LO! THE BIRD HAS FALLEN'.

MARY is sitting on a tree stump, eyes closed, playing the guitar and singing in a trance like state.

MARY
(sings)
Three cheers for Master Edward,
Who fought a doughty fight,

F/X SHOT: The strange coils of glowing foam are bubbling up from the well spring.

F/X SHOT: C.U. on the strange illuminated foam.

DISSOLVE TO:

INT. - STUDIO CONTROL ROOM - DAY

GRAMS: 'LO! THE BIRD HAS FALLEN'.

MARY (V.O.)
(sings)
When the rebels from Preston,
He drove in headlong flight...

CLARE switches off the reel to reel. However, the sound of Mary's singing continues! CLARE stares in disbelief at the reel to reel player. She fiddles with the controls, but Mary's singing continues to fill the room. CLARE rushes around switching everything off, but, still the singing continues.

CLARE
Shut up, shut up!!

Mary's singing rolls on. CLARE covers her ears in fear. The song continues.

MARY (V.O.)
(sings)
Two salvoes true and mighty,
Rang from his sportsman's gun...

CUT TO:

INT. - ABANDONED BARN - DAY

PATRICK, DOUGLAS, DAVIE and ARTHUR still stand around the apparition of the burning WITCH.

WITCH

I forgive you. Now please, forgive yourselves.

After a moment's hesitation, PATRICK nods then walks 'into' the WITCH. As he does so, PATRICK dissolves into a puff of dark dust. One after the other, DOUGLAS, DAVIE and ARTHUR walk 'into' the WITCH and each one of them disappears in a burst of dust.

The WITCH blazes even more brightly for a moment, then she's gone.

HARD CUT TO:

EXT. - YARD - DAY

MARK and PETER are waiting to be picked up. MARK smokes a cigarette, PETER texts on his mobile and rubs his cheek where his tooth is aching. The mood is not great.

MARK

Is he on his fucking way or what?

PETER

(reads text)

Says he'll be here in 5 minutes.

MARK

Thank fuck for that!

MARK looks across the yard. Something catches his eye.

CUT TO REVEAL a forlorn looking MACFISK, standing at the entrance to the yard.

MARK's POV: As MACFISK walks across the yard towards them, the surroundings seem to phase in and out of register. MACFISK walks up close to MARK.

Suddenly - as happened earlier in the barn - an area of glistening light separates MARK and MACFISK from the rest of the yard. Through the light we can make out the oblivious Peter fiddling with his mobile. MARK addresses MACFISK in a friendly manner, seemingly unconcerned by the supernatural circumstances.

MARK (CONT'D)
You alright cock?

MACFISK
(shakes his head)
Everything's wrong. I'm away home.

MARK
Me too. Probably for the best.

MACFISK stares at him for a moment.

MACFISK
We don't win do we? The Jacobites.

MARK
(shakes his head)
No. Yer come close though. For a while the Whigs are shitting themselves. But no. After the Battle of Preston, the Jacobites dissipate.

MACFISK
(nods)
Aye. I thought so.

CUT TO:

INT. - STUDIO CONTROL ROOM - DAY

GRAMS: MARY 'LO! THE BIRD HAS FALLEN'.

CLARE is slouched in her swivel chair, head in hands. The song continues to play.

MARY (V.O.)
(sings)
And lo! The bird is fallen,
Raised cheers from everyone...

F/X SHOT: Unseen by CLARE, the strange glowing foam starts to bubble out of the speakers in serpentine coils.

HARD CUT TO:

EXT. - YARD - DAY

MARK and MACFISK are still standing within the dome of light. The oblivious PETER remains outside the dome texting.

MARK
You should go.

MACFISK
I wanted to fight, because I saw injustice against the ordinary folk o' the land.

MARK
(nods)
It gets a lot fucking worse actually. Better not to know.

MACFISK

Aye, I reckon you're right.

MARK and MACFISK shake hands.

MARK

All the best pal.

The dome of light disappears. MACFISK turns around and walks away, clambers over the wall and starts making his way up the hill.

PETER

My toothache's eased off.

MARK

Good.

Ed's car drives up through the entrance and into the yard.

MARK glances about the place, shakes his head and mutters to himself.

MARK (CONT'D)

Fuckin' countryside...

MARK and PETER get into the car. The car doors slam.

Ed's car pulls away. As it does so, we see MARK glance back at the studio, his face framed in the passenger window.

FREEZE FRAME.

DISSOLVE TO:

EXT - HILL - DAY

MACFISK looks down at Clare's farmhouse from a distance.

MACFISK's POV: He surveys the landscape. He sees Ed's car wind its way down the road. Then JEFF and BEV approaching on a motorbike. The two vehicles pass each other.

MACFISK turns and continues to walk up the hill. We linger on his departing figure, disappearing into the landscape.

DISSOLVE TO:

EXT. - YARD - DAY

JEFF drives the motorbike into the YARD with BEV riding on the back. They dismount.

DISSOLVE TO:

INT. - STUDIO CONTROL ROOM - DAY

JIB SHOT: We are looking down into the studio. CLARE is slumped over the mixing desk. Enter JEFF followed by BEV.

TIGHT SHOT ON JEFF and BEV. They come to a halt, nervous about going forward, uncertain if she's alive or dead.

BEV

Clare?

To their relief, CLARE sits up. She turns around and smiles at them.

JEFF and BEV smile back in relief.

CLARE's smile goes on too long. Her eyes are glassy and dark. Her mind has gone. She lifts her hand up to her mouth. It is covered in the strange yellow/grey mucus-like growth. CLARE's empty smile widens, then she begins to gnaw on the strange growth on her hand.

CUT TO BLACK:

GRAMS: 'HOT CAKE' BY THE FALL (00.00).

END CREDITS.

THE INEXPLICABLE 1 & 2

The Original TV Pitches

T H E   I N E X P L I C A B L E

A Supernatural Anthology Series for TV

Written by

MARK E. SMITH & GRAHAM DUFF

6x30 minutes

INEXPLICABLE is a series of macabre, humorous and gripping stories of modern day hauntings, premonitions and possession set in and around the North West of England.

Each week the lead role is played by a different guest star. (Casting ideas include Craig Cash, Jane Horrocks and Mark Gatiss).

Bringing a perverse sense of humour to the classic tradition of shows such as 'The Twilight Zone', the BBC's M.R. James adaptations and Nigel Kneale's 'Beasts', **INEXPLICABLE** serves up a unique blend of comic terror…

'IT'S A BETTER LIFE HERE'

Jim and Sue are a pair of aging scallies determined to turn their backs on their old life of petty crime. They move out of Moss Side, away from all the violence, the drugs and the gangsters and relocate to the quiet, picturesque Pendle village of Marswell. Initially, it seems like the perfect place for the couple to start their life afresh. However, Jim and Sue quickly find themselves hankering for their old city life as they fall foul of vicious foxes, a mentally unbalanced single mum and a neighbour who runs his own satanic neo-fascist group.

'THE KALLENS'

In a dilapidated Prestwich mental ward, Mr Grant, an aging delusional paranoiac, watches a TV news report as a certain Leith Kallen is made Prime Minister. The news is seemingly enough to send Grant into a fit. As a Staff Nurse struggles to restrain him, we flash back through Grant's life in five yearly intervals, the story unfolding in reverse. All through his life Grant has repeatedly encountered the self serving and sinister Kallen. And each time Kallen has loomed up, he has been the harbinger of chaos. But surely you can't be haunted by someone who isn't dead? Only when we finally flash back to Grant and Kallen's first ever meeting do we understand the terrible truth.

'VACANT POSSESSION'

The Breakspeare is a huge 18th century edifice in the heart of Manchester. Originally it was a massive sweatshop, with adults and children kept in inhuman conditions, toiling endlessly for a pittance. Today however, it's just another building converted into luxury apartments for wealthy professionals - like Susan and Marsha; a lesbian couple in the process of setting up a designer furniture store - who adore the Breakspeare's old world charm. But the ghosts of the Industrial Revolution are about to rise up and turn Susan and Marsha's life into a living hell.

'NO ORDINARY ANGEL'

Jeff Maxwell is a weak-willed simpleton, bullied into joining the local chapter of the Hells Angels by his Neanderthal elder brother Mick. Forever the butt of the gang's taunts and nasty practical jokes, Jeff retreats into a Walter Mitty style dream world. In his fantasies, Jeff is a charismatic biker, pulling gorgeous chicks and effortlessly beating his enemies to a pulp, as his own warped Russ Meyer style voice-over narrates his exploits. But when Jeff survives a near fatal crash, he finds fantasy and reality begin to merge, as his 'narrator' starts telling him to kill and kill again.

'THE DEATH OF STANDARDS'

On his way to work, a council health and safety official deliberately knocks over a pedestrian and drives on. Bizarrely, upon arriving at his office he launches into a heartfelt tirade against hit and run drivers. Meanwhile, the department's team leader instigates a series of compulsory redundancies then appears on a local TV news programme to protest against the sackings in the strongest possible terms. Strangely, Jenny Carver - working as a temp in the office - seems to be the only one aware of her colleagues' paradoxical behaviour. Finding herself trapped in a world where everybody really is their own worst enemy, she begins to suspect there may be some kind of supernatural intelligence at work.

'TAPE LOOP'

Des is the ever optimistic owner of The Loop - a tiny, grotty recording studio in Cheetham Hill. The place is so damp and out-dated, nobody's used it for years. Yet, when an old novelty single which was recorded there is re-released it becomes a surprise number one hit. Suddenly Des is besieged by bands wanting to book the studio in order to get "that Loop sound". And that's just what they get - no matter what is recorded there, it ends up sounding like the irritating novelty single. Whilst Des is initially amused, he begins to realise that the very fabric of the studio is impregnated with a malignant viral madness…

T H E   I N E X P L I C A B L E

A Supernatural Anthology Series for TV

Written by

GRAHAM DUFF & MARK E. SMITH

6x30 minutes

Jeff Sherwin is a hapless Lancashire electrician whose life is going nowhere. Weak willed and disillusioned with his lot, Jeff frequently retreats into his various fantasy worlds.

However, what the dozy Jeff continually fails to comprehend, is that his real life is already plagued by the fantastical. As he daydreams his way through the day, Jeff is oblivious of the fact he's an absolute magnet for the uncanny, the paranormal and the downright frightening.

Having recently split up with his girlfriend, Jeff is temporarily lodging with his sister Claire and her husband Len - an obnoxious oaf and leader of a small Hells Angels style biker gang by the name of Satan's Stooges. Meanwhile, the long suffering Claire runs a shabby, out-moded recording studio with a dark secret.

Jeff dutifully pays weekly visits to his dad - a delusional paranoiac, confined to a Prestwich mental home. He is morbidly obsessed by a certain Mr Kallen, a former acquaintance and TV pundit who is, according to Jeff's dad, "secretly controlling everything". Jeff dismisses this as nonsense. But should he?

A winning mix of biting character comedy, bizarre and inventive plots and genuinely chilling set pieces, INEXPLICABLE is a unique show which provides the missing link between *The Twilight Zone* and *Billy Liar*.

Ep.1 - 'VACANT POSSESSION'

Jeff is doing some rewiring at The Breakspeare - a huge 18th century edifice in the heart of Manchester. Originally a sweatshop - with adults and children toiling in inhuman conditions for a pittance – today it's been converted into luxury apartments for wealthy professionals. Jeff is working in the flat of Susan and Ella; a lesbian couple who run a designer furniture store. He fantasises about living in a menage a trois with the two women, blissfully unaware that the ghosts of the Industrial Revolution are about to rise up and turn life into a living hell…

Ep.2 – 'THE JUDGES'

Jeff becomes convinced that – unlike the shambolic bands he sees Claire working with at the recording studio – he has real potential as a singer. So, when TV talent show 'Star Catcher' holds auditions in town, Jeff just has to give it a go. However, once in front of the judges it becomes apparent he's completely lacking in confidence and charisma and can barely hold a tune. Yet strangely, the judges – three oddly wizened individuals – choose Jeff to go through to the next round. What Jeff doesn't suspect, is that the judges are vampiric beings who sustain themselves by feeding on the energy and enthusiasm of the wannabes…

Ep.3 – 'TAPE LOOP'

Jeff does some work for his sister Claire at 'The Loop', her grotty and out-moded recording studio. As usual, business is slow, so Jeff has plenty of time to daydream about being a big shot producer. However, when a novelty single recorded at the studio shoots to number one, Claire receives a flood of calls from people who want "that Loop sound". And that's exactly what they get. Because no matter how many times Claire replaces the tapes or Jeff rechecks the equipment, it seems that every piece of music they record ends up sounding like the irritating novelty single. It's enough to drive someone mad…

Ep.4 – 'THE DEATH OF STANDARDS'

Jeff is doing some electrical work at the council health and safety office and fantasising about running the council. Meanwhile, one of the council officials is driving to work when she deliberately knocks over a pedestrian and drives on. Bizarrely, upon arriving at the office, she launches into a heartfelt tirade against hit and run drivers. That same day, the department's team leader makes a series of compulsory redundancies then appears on the local news protesting against the sackings in the strongest possible terms. Although Jeff doesn't realise it, this is a world where everybody really is their own worst enemy. And it seems some kind of supernatural intelligence is at work…

Ep.5 – 'NO ORDINARY ANGEL'

Against his better judgement, Jeff allows brother-in-law Len to bully him into joining Satan's Stooges. Inevitably, Jeff becomes the butt of the gang's taunts and nasty practical jokes. Retreating into his dream world, Jeff imagines himself to be a charismatic biker. In his fantasies, we see Jeff pulling gorgeous chicks and effortlessly beating up his enemies, as a warped Russ Meyer style voice-over narrates his exploits. However, when Jeff survives a near fatal crash without a scratch, he finds fantasy and reality begin to merge, as his 'narrator' starts telling him to kill and kill again…

Ep.6 – 'IT'S A BETTER LIFE HERE'

Determined to make a fresh start, Jeff moves out of the city and away from the bikers and the violence. Relocating to a cottage in the picturesque, leafy Pendle village of Marswell, Jeff fantasises about cultivating a huge ornate garden. Back in the real world, Jeff is kindling a romance with Beth – an attractive single mum who lives next door. What he fails to grasp, is Beth is the priestess of a local satanic neo-fascist coven. And there's also the problem of the ancient standing stone which refuses to stay in one place…

REAL, ASSUMED OR IMAGINARY

It has been remarked by numerous observers on numerous occasions, that in a different life Mark E. Smith would have made a superb short story writer. This assertion is easily borne out by even a cursory perusal of his lyrics. He was an inventive and idiosyncratic writer, and when it came to narratives, a supremely economic storyteller.

The symbolist poet Paul Verlaine is reputed to have said, "The surest way to be a bore, is to tell the whole story". As a lyricist Mark understood this notion implicitly. He knew how to edit an idea down to its essential elements.

Importantly, he was also an experimentalist. Even his most narratively cohesive texts are still prone to abstraction. There is a genuine feel of collage in much of his work. But he didn't arrive at this via an act of physical collage, or by the application of Brion Gysin and William Burroughs's cut-up or fold-in techniques. Rather Mark would engage in multiple trains of thought. As he wrote in the sleeve notes for the album *Perverted by Language*: 'Smith applied cut-up technique literally to brain'.

He also stated on more than one occasion that he used something he referred to as 'clang process'. This apparently involved creating an association of ideas by speaking sentences thick with assonance, homophones or near homophones – we can hear examples of this in titles such as 'Antidotes+Anecdotes', 'Gibbus Gibson' and *Pander! Panda! Panzer!* In reality of course, we actually know very little about how he composed his texts. Because, as Mark often remarked, he didn't like to give away his secrets.

Over the following pages, I've chosen to focus on 25 sets of Mark's lyrics – five from each decade of The Fall's existence. I believe each of them, in their different ways, serves to illustrate Mark's skills as a storyteller. There are horror stories, tales of time travel, natural disaster, uprising, possession, mind transference and a lurid assembly of hideous supernatural beings.

Obviously I'm not for a moment suggesting that reading Mark's lyrics as short stories is the correct way, or even the best way to experience them. What is undeniable however, is that so many of them certainly can be enjoyed as narrative. But let's be clear, the majority of the texts cited here – with a few exceptions such as 'The N.W.R.A.' – were created as *lyrics* to be sung within a rock and roll song. A form driven by primal energies and beats, a form where the '*Hey!*'s and the '*Ba-ba-bah!*'s are often far more crucial than any amount of smart wordsmithery.

Mark was equally capable of creating anti-narrative. His fascination with the texts of the vorticist artist Wyndham Lewis undoubtedly played a part in his creation of lyrics that operated as a series of declarations. Lewis's literary magazine *Blast* ran for just two issues between 1914 and 1915 and his bold typographic arrangements of terse, splenetic texts seem to shout off of the page. It's impossible to see lines by Lewis such as '*Curse with Expletive of Whirlwind, the Britannic Aesthete*' and not be reminded of Mark's own elliptical pronouncements.

Although he usually took a remarkable amount of care with his lyrics, the odd phrase aside, he never wanted them printed on The Fall's album sleeves. He strongly believed the words shouldn't be divorced from the music. However, a description that comes up again and again, whenever The Fall's lyrics are under discussion, is 'cryptic'. And when an artist produces cryptic work, it naturally follows that a portion of the audience will feel compelled to decrypt. Yet Mark wanted it both ways. He wanted the freedom to create texts liberally threaded with references to ideas, films, music and literature: from classic to esoteric, from popular to pulp. But he also actively discouraged the unpicking of any of those threads.

Like Allen Ginsberg, with his claim of "first thought, best thought", Mark had an obsession with immediacy. He never wanted to do exactly the same thing twice. He preferred to get something down and move on. Not because he wasn't deeply invested in the idea. He was. But he was even more deeply invested in the *next* idea. Mark wasn't interested in hanging around to polish or pick over what he'd just done. So he couldn't really understand why anyone else would want to.

In Mick Middles's insightful and extremely readable book *The Fall* published in 2003, Mark told the author, "There's some fucking professor in America who teaches about the meaning of Fall songs. I mean, can you believe that? The whole point is to understand and move on. Not hold seminars or open fucking web pages."

But of course the instant an artist puts a piece of work out in the world is also the exact moment they lose control of how it is perceived. And perceptions of The Fall's work are polarized. Some dismiss the group as an ugly, barely intelligible mess. Whilst for others, The Fall demand the same kind of investigation, research and respect accorded to the work of James Joyce or Stanley Kubrick.

Although Mark was keen to project an image of disdain towards 'scholars' of his lyrics, and resolutely refused to provide any assistance in the 'decoding' of his work, I believe he was secretly proud that his lyrics were the subject of such debate and confusion.

His texts are especially fascinating for their inclusion of other fictional worlds, such as those created by H.P. Lovecraft, M.R. James, Edgar Allan Poe, Roger Corman, Ursula K. Le Guin, Philip K. Dick, Marvel comics and so on. Once you begin to scratch away at Mark's lyrics, you are quickly drawn into an expansive web of references, allusions, quotes, influences and connections.

'A literature defined by unreliable narration, impossible plots, fragmentation, paranoia, inclusion of other fictions, authorial self reference and the erasure of the distinction between high and low culture.'

A description of Mark's writings? No: a definition of Postmodernist literature. Whilst Mark would have surely deplored the observation, it cannot be denied that his lyrics display all the hallmarks of the Postmodern. However, it seems entirely possible that this is something he arrived at via his own instinctive feel for how he wanted to assemble information and communicate it to others.

Mark frequently pointed out that he often wrote from the viewpoint of a character, rather than as himself. Perversely, he would then sometimes insert himself, or altered versions of his persona, into the narratives, alongside friends and other elements from his personal life. At times he would use verbatim texts he'd encountered, be they lines from films, books, magazine articles, advertising copy, other people's songs or his own songs. This innate sense of collage is at the very heart of so much of Mark's best work.

By the time of his death, he had been writing lyrics for over forty years. The earliest text cited here is 'Futures and Pasts', which was written in 1976. Whereas the final 'Couples vs. Jobless Mid 30s' was composed in 2017. It's tempting to say that over the decades Mark had been evolving his style. But in reality his unique manner of using words and crafting narrative arrived fully formed at the very start of his career.

Listen to the earliest recordings of The Fall, and you can hear that lyrically everything is already manifest: the down to earth North Western cynicism mixed with science fiction concepts, ideas borrowed and repurposed from classic gothic literature, a fascination with heightened states, psychic energies and multiple time lines, an ear for unusual turns of phrase, archaic words and attention grabbing word clusters, an eye for unlikely characters and a propensity for divergent storylines.

During the last decade of The Fall's existence, aware that he had come to be viewed by some as a kind of post punk poet laureate, Mark elected to short circuit matters. His vocal delivery had always been rich in character, low in musicality, but now it became ever more raw and untamed. Here was rock and roll vocalization rooted in the guttural delivery of Don Van Vliet, but delivered with such vitriolic force it seemed to share a currency with the savage ululations of Diamanda Galas. It was as if unintelligibility had become an aim.

Yet, even as he was ruthlessly cutting back on both his word count and his clarity, Mark could not help but generate texts which still bristled with narrative hooks, improbable connections and intriguing references.

I should emphasise that I'm not claiming the following 25 examples represent the very best Fall *songs*. Although I would venture that at least some of them do. Rather, my intention is to discuss what I consider to be some of Mark's finest *texts*, purely in terms of how they operate as narrative fiction. What I offer here are of course merely my own interpretations. Other equally valid perspectives are most certainly available.

I should also mention that I am in no way suggesting that Mark's lyrics can be decoded in a way that reveals all their secrets and hidden meanings. They can't. Because impenetrability was hard wired into their very construction. Not even Mark himself knew the true meaning of all his words. Whilst some of his lyrics or sections of lyrics were keenly crafted, others were the result of him speaking off the top of his head. He would then transcribe his words from recordings. These might be used pretty much verbatim, or cut in with other more structured ideas.

He also included lines or phrases that were deliberately meaningless.

"I always try and put a little crack in it," Mark remarked, in a 1984 interview for the book *Tape Delay*. "And I always try and put lyrics that mean nothing and like jumble it all up".

So it's not simply a case of lyrics that invite multiple readings. It's actually a case of lyrics that cannot have one definitive reading, because any absolute sense was hidden even from their creator. Consequently, you may take it as read that what follows barely scratches the surface.

If nothing else, I hope this encourages you to go online and read Mark's words in isolation. At the end of each entry, I've picked out a key line from the text that I believe demonstrates the fact you are in the hands of a master storyteller.

By the way, I am perfectly aware that the main purpose of these kinds of assertions and lists is to provide the reader with something to disagree with.

▲ ▲ ▲

THE 1970S

'Futures and Pasts'

One of the three earliest complete lyrics Mark wrote in 1976 (along with 'Repetition' and 'Oh! Brother'). It's a series of narrative fragments that begins with the arresting lines *'I was in a sleeping dream, when a policeman brought my mother home'*. This feels like a traumatic image from childhood: *'I didn't scream, I was too old for that.'*

Then it spins into a drunken dream experienced much later in life. It's almost as if the narrator is seeing the same policeman again, but this time he's lost in a fog. It might be the fog of time, or could it be some kind of supernatural occurrence? Certainly the repeated line *'I understand but I don't see it'* is suggestive of a connection with a presence or energy that is beyond normal perception.

The narrator remarks that he is able to read the faces of men and women much older than he, and divine the secrets of their lives. Mark often stated that he could read people by their faces. The text also contains the earliest lyrical example of his distrust of nostalgia, when he remarks that if someone is pining for their childhood, they should remind themselves how much they hated it at the time.

KEY LINE: *'At the bottom of the street it seemed there was a policeman lost in the fog.'*

'Various Times'

Here is another early example of Mark's fascination with temporality as a narrative device. There are three different time zones in the story. Firstly the past: Germany in 1940, where a disaffected youth becomes a guard at Belsen concentration camp, and witnesses *'An old Jew's face dripping red.'*

Then we're in the present: 1978. Following a report of a snippet of private conversation, the narrator informs us that he has a deep disdain for conformity and is planning to drop out of society.

Next we're in the future, in the year *'one nine eighty.'* This is a dystopian future, a bombsite of *'black windows and smoky holes.'* A wounded man drinks weak beer in a world where they have *'got rid of time.'* It seems time itself has become navigable, as we're informed that Dr Doom has just got back from the Salem witch trials of the 1690s. This is a nod to the 1976 Spider-man story featured in the comic *Marvel Team-Up* (issues 41–44) involving time travel, super-villain Dr Doom and the Scarlet Witch, partially set during the witch trials.

The lyric also makes a telling reference to Ursula K. Le Guin's 1971 science fiction novel *The Lathe of Heaven*. In the book, a man named George Orr is capable of creating a special energy in his dream state. This power is harnessed by a well-meaning scientist to change reality itself. Orr dreams up alternate worlds, yet each is more problematic than the last. For example, when Orr is instructed to dream of a world without racism, it turns the skin of the entire world's population a uniform grey.

Mark remarked that he'd felt proud of the lyric to 'Various Times' when he wrote it, and perhaps surprisingly that the structure had been inspired by the Shangri-Las' 1966 single 'Past, Present and Future'.

KEY LINE: *'But I'm the sort that gets out the bath with a dirty face.'*

'A Figure Walks'

Like the writings of M.R. James, this tale of mounting dread concerns the horror that may lurk just out of the corner of your eye. Indeed, the title itself sounds like it belongs in a compendium of James's short stories. Mark stated that it was "written during a long walk home wearing an anorak which restricted vision by two thirds." The notion that it was an anorak, that most drab and quotidian of garments, which initiated the creeping unease is typical of Mark's sense of the macabre hiding behind banality.

The narrator's fear that the figure may kill him leads to the line *'A quick trip to the ice house.'* This is suggestive of a mortuary where the corpses are kept at a very low temperature. It's also possibly a reference to the 1978 BBC1 television ghost story for Christmas *The Ice House*. The drama, which had aired just a few weeks before

'A Figure Walks' received its on-stage debut, concerns a series of strange disappearances at a health spa.

Meanwhile, the narrator's description of the figure itself is deeply unpleasant: *'It's got eyes of brown, watery, nails of pointed yellow, hands of black carpet.'* In an interview with the *NME*, Mark stated that the figure was in fact a monster from outer space.

"I think of it as my big Stephen King outing."

KEY LINE: *'Thought brought the drought about.'*

'Flat of Angles'

Mark described this as "an objective story song", whilst his sleeve notes to the *Dragnet* album state "It's about the criminal elements who have no choice whether to go out or stay in. Reminds us of tea and *The Daily Mirror*."

A man who has murdered his wife is hiding out in a small rented room. His father-in-law appears in a newspaper, holding up a photo of him. The murderer knows the police are closing in. The line *'His veins are full of evil serum'* hints that he may also be injecting narcotics. He spends his days surrounded by dirty laundry, watching soap operas, feeling increasingly oppressed by the claustrophobic angles of the flat.

Perhaps like Walter Gilman, the protagonist in H.P. Lovecraft's 1932 story *The Dreams in the Witch House*, the murderer's sanity is being tested by his rented loft apartment's strange geometry. There is also a suggestion of defeat in the title. As in: 'I'm flat out of angles.' Finally, the murderer is tempted outside by the sunshine, but by now his paranoia has become all-consuming.

The use within the lyric of the word *'Dragnet'* (also the title of a US TV crime show that had aired in the UK during Mark's youth) is a reminder that although his work would always retain a distinct flavour of the North West of England, Mark was far from immune to American influences. Indeed this narrative could be said to play out like an episode of *The Twilight Zone*.

KEY LINE: *'The streets are full of mercenary eyes.'*

'Spectre vs. Rector'

This is one of Mark's most remarkable texts, and it opens with an incantation and exhortation. It calls upon the horror authors M.R. James and Peter Van Greenaway and exploitation film producer Roger Corman, as well as Ray Milland, star of Corman's adaptation of Edgar Allan Poe's *Premature Burial.* But perhaps most significantly, it also calls upon Yog-Sothoth. In the mythos of H.P. Lovecraft Yog-Sothoth is the all-seeing ancient god locked outside the universe.

What follows is the story of a Hampshire Rector possessed by a spectre. When the rector receives a visit from a detective, things take a violent turn. The detective struggles with the rector, who is under the control of the spectre. As the detective is blown against the wall, the spectre revels in its own power, uttering the words *'I've waited since Caesar for this!'* This tells us the evil is a very ancient force indeed.

An unnamed hero arrives, an exorcist who claims to have *'saved a thousand lives'*. In the tumult, the spectre enters the exorcist, but *'the possession is ineffectual.'* By the end, all we know for sure is the rector has died, the detective (now referred to as the inspector) has been *'driven half insane'*, and the exhausted exorcist has retreated to the hills. The whereabouts of the spectre are unknown.

Crucially, we have been made aware that the story is incomplete. After all, the different sections are titled Part One, Part Two, Part Four, Scene Five, Part Six and Last Scene. Like the narrator in M.R. James's 'Count Magnus', we have been presented with a body of documentation from which we must piece together an understanding of what has transpired.

KEY LINE: *'The rector lived in Hampshire, the spectre was from Chorazina.'**

* *The city of Chorazina is referred to in M.R. James's 'Count Mangus' as being the potential birthplace for the antichrist. The sleeve notes to the* Dragnet *album refer to Chorazina as being 'Negative Jerusalem.'*

THE 1980S

'New Face in Hell'

'New Face in Hell' comes over like a highly compressed Graham Greene short story. In fact this is probably Mark's most straightforward narrative text. A wireless enthusiast – most likely a man operating a CB radio – finds himself unexpectedly listening in on a government plot. He decides to call on his neighbour and inform him of his discovery.

The description of the wireless enthusiast being *'secretly excited'*, as he wants *'friendship and favour of'* his neighbour may imply that he's hopeful for a romantic or erotic relationship. The neighbor is also described as *'a hunter'*.** However, upon arrival next door, the wireless enthusiast discovers his neighbour has been poisoned.

As *'a prickly line of sweat covers enthusiast's forehead'*, he experiences the realisation that his neighbour has been killed by government agents. There is something especially pleasing here, in the description of he and his neighbour having talked of the government *'on cream porches.'* Within moments, a government agent has arrived and arrested the wireless enthusiast. He is being framed for the death.

Although the story has a satisfying conclusion, it definitely feels like we are only being shown a couple of scenes from the middle of a much wider narrative. What happened in the lead up to the events described? And what will ensue now the wireless enthusiast must stand trial?

KEY LINE: *'A muscular, thick skinned, slit-eyed neighbour is at the table.'*

** *Another stand out narrative lyric from this era also features a hunter: 'Jawbone and the Air-Rifle' is the tale of a 'rabbit killer' who falls victim to an ancient curse.*

'Impression of J. Temperance'

This is a horror story, in which interspecies breeding results in a frightening abomination. A local dog breeder, by the name of Jermyn Temperance, is treated with hatred by almost everyone. He has intercourse with a bitch and, when it goes into labour, he calls Cameron, a vet and one of Temperance's only two friends. The bitch gives birth to a hideous hybrid being, causing the vet to flee and phone his wife in terror.

In many ways, the new-born being resembles Temperance, yet its rat-like features render it horrifying. *'The next bit is hard to relate'* says Mark. But the mention of *'brown sockets, purple eyes'* tells us something is dreadfully wrong.

The story's final lines are a classic example of unresolved horror: the creature simply slips out the door: the nightmare will continue. As a keen fan of H.P. Lovecraft, it seems highly likely that Mark took the name Jermyn from Lovecraft's 1920 story *The Facts Concerning The Late Arthur Jermyn and His Family*, in which the 'hero' discovers that he himself is a descendant of interspecies breeding.

KEY LINE: *'His hideous replica, scrutinised little monster, disappeared through the door.'*

'The N.W.R.A.'

This is the closing piece on The Fall's *Grotesque* album, a collection that saw Mark's storytelling skills take centre stage. 'The N.W.R.A.' (*'The North Will Rise Again'*) is his longest narrative text, and certainly his most detailed, including sequences in Soho, Manchester, Darlington, Newcastle, Teesside Docks and Edinburgh.

The story concerns a mass uprising in the North of England, and the narrator (at least initially) is one Joe Totale, who describes himself as the *'yet unborn son'* of Roman Totale XVII. This would seem to indicate the narrative is a vision of future events, related from the perspective of either a fetus or a disembodied spirit.

Mark had previously used the character of Roman Totale XVII to write the sleeve notes for The Fall's live album *Totale's Turns (It's*

Now Or Never) and the single 'Fiery Jack'. The character had also appeared in that song's B-side 'Second Dark Age', where he is referred to as *'The bastard offspring of Charles I and the Great God Pan'*. *The Great God Pan* is also the title of a novella by the Welsh horror writer Arthur Machen, whom Mark was a great admirer of.

The northern uprising itself is doomed to *'turn out wrong'* when a business acquaintance of Totale by the name of Tony becomes involved and corrupts the cause. This may well be a joking reference to Factory Records' director Tony Wilson.

In one particularly vivid scene, we learn R. Totale is hiding out underground, wearing an ostrich mask. The description also includes the lines *'body a tentacle mess.'* Once again, this cannot help but summon thoughts of the creatures of H.P. Lovecraft, whilst confirming that Totale is not human in origin.

KEY LINE: *'The Arndale had been razed, shop staff knocked off their ladders, security guards hung from moving escalators.'*

'Winter (Hostel-Maxi)'

A tale of spiritual possession, described in the press release for the *Hex Enduction Hour* album as concerning "an insane child who is taken over by a spirit from the mind of a cooped-up alcoholic, and his ravaged viewpoints and theories."

The narrator witnesses the child – referred to only as *'The mad kid'* – walking with his mother, who is a cleaning lady, accompanied by their large, black dog. As they pass *'the alcoholics's dry-out house'*, the boy becomes agitated, demanding to be given the dog's lead. The narrator recalls how, two weeks earlier, the mad kid had spoken aggressively to he and a friend, shouting *"I'll take both of you on!"*

In the dry-out house, an alcoholic named Manny is being pressured into putting on a medallion. It may be in recognition of his attempts to stay sober, although, as we were informed earlier that Manny is *'working off his hangover'* it seems more likely that the medallion is some kind of magickal artifact designed to initiate the spiritual transference. Either way *'His soul went out of window, over the lawn and ran into the mad kid.'*

Despite the observation that the child has returned from the *'backwards kids' party'* the narrator acknowledges he may well be a genius: *'The mad kid had 4 lights. The average is 2.5 lights.'*

Fall drummer Karl Burns has claimed that the 'mad kid' referred to a boy who had offered to take on both he and Mark in a fight. If this is to be believed, then it seems possible that Mark was rationalising the two outbursts he had witnessed: the offer of a fight and the demand to be given the dog's lead, as the moments when the boy was taken over by the ravaged spirit of an alcoholic.

KEY LINE: *'There was a feminist's Austin Maxi parked outside, with anti-nicotine, anti-nuclear stickers on the side.'*

'Wings'

Here is another tale set in more than one time zone. The narrator accidentally acquires the ability to travel through time, when he purchases *'a pair of flabby wings'* – a phrase ripe with Lovecraftian revulsion.

'There is a list of incorrect things' he reveals. This notion of a gathering of wrong information is surely suggestive of Lovecraft's fictional grimoire *The Necronomicon*. Yet it is the spirit of Arthur Machen that is summoned with the lines *'Hovered mid-air outside a study. An academic kneaded his chin.'*

The narrator enlists the help of some gremlins, to interfere with the airline routes. This notion may have been inspired by the famous *Twilight Zone* episode 'Nightmare at 20,000 Feet' involving a man on an airline flight, who keeps seeing a hideous gremlin interfering with the wing of the plane.

In Mark's story, the narrator then pays off the gremlins with '*stuffing from my wings*'. However, this causes him to hit a *'time lock'* and be transported to the 1860s, where he states he's been trapped for 125 years – so presumably he is no longer a victim of the aging process. He becomes involved in a shootout with *'some veterans from the US Civil War.'* Once again he hits a time lock, and returns to the present day.

Unfortunately, he discovers *'The place I made the purchase no longer exists.'* He realises that it is his own actions in the past that caused the shop to be erased. Now he is doomed to live out his time, hiding away from nosy kids with *'wings [that] rot and curl right under me.'*

There are numerous examples in science fiction of a time traveller whose behaviour in the past leads to their doom in the present. Indeed it's one of the key paradigms of the time travel narrative. A number of influential authors produced short stories around the subject, including John Wyndham's *Wanderers of Time*, Stanislaw Lem's 'The Twentieth Voyage' and Ray Bradbury's 'A Sound of Thunder'.

In terms of 'Wings' itself, I feel compelled to throw two further possible influences into the mix. Firstly, the 1963 *Twilight Zone* episode: 'No Time Like The Past' – wherein a time traveller attempts to prevent the major conflicts of history. Secondly, the 1965 *Doctor Who* serial: 'The Time Meddler'. The titular character is a time traveller who has a list of wrong things, and interferes in historic battles. The story also features a character bemoaning the fact he lacks wings.

KEY LINE: *'A small alteration of the past can turn time into space.'*

THE 1990S

'Sing! Harpy'

The opening line *'The harpy was tops'* initially appears an unlikely construct. The contrast of the menace inherent in the word 'harpy' with the almost giddy 'tops' seems like it can only be intended ironically. Yet the operative word here is *'was'*. For this appears to be a story of falling out of love, related in part as a struggle with a mythic being.

At times, the language is rooted in a more traditionally romantic mode of expression (*'She left the moors behind her, and the beige heather'*) and the narrator states how initially the woman was *'without malice'* and *'just too good in bed'*. But eventually he becomes concerned, feeling she is gripping him like a hawk.

It should not go unnoted that Mark's first wife and Fall guitarist Brix Smith later came to believe the lyrics were about her. Certainly the references to the harpy having a show business background, and the confidence to *'sell you anything'* support this reading.

But, as is almost always the case with Mark's texts, there is more than one form of narrative in operation here. Whilst the talk of talons etc. may be metaphorical, the supernatural cannot be ruled out. There is the possibility that the character involved is not 100% human, or that she may indeed be an actual harpy from the ancient myths of Greece: the beings Ovid called 'human-vultures', with the body of a woman and the wings and claws of a bird of prey.

KEY LINE: *'Her talons were quite famished.'*

*'Paranoia Man in Cheap Sh*t Room'*

In some ways, the story here resembles that of 'Flat of Angles'. A mentally unstable protagonist spends the majority of his time holed up in a (presumably) rented room. And, when he does venture into the outside world, he is not equal to the task. He *'Shakes in the chemists'* and suffers from *'drooped mental inertia.'*

It's interesting that despite his extreme neurotic state the man is described as being *'at the zenith of his powers.'* Maybe this is why, rather than being referred to as a 'paranoid man', he is called *'Paranoia Man'*. Perhaps he is in fact some kind of superhero of paranoia.

The title and some of the story itself is refashioned from the 1960 *Twilight Zone* episode 'Nervous Man in a Four Dollar Room'. In Rod Serling's original story, a criminal checks into a cheap hotel room. He has been given a gun and informed that the following day he must murder a barkeeper. He then spends a night of reckoning, talking to an alternate version of his self in the room's mirror. This may well be the origin of the repeated phrase *'replica shooter.'*

KEY LINE: *'Puts his head down when girls pass in the street.'*

'Service'

On the surface, the emotions and actions expressed here are pretty much the opposite of those in 'Paranoia Man in Cheap Sh*t Room' – the piece which precedes 'Service' on the album *The Infotainment Scan*. Whereas that tale told of a man almost too paranoid to mix with society, this piece recounts the experience of someone undertaking a pleasant walk, during which he kicks leaves and fallen branches. He is walking in winter, and quite possibly in the winter of his own life.

However, the sudden insertion of the phrase *'Thought transference'* suggests that the person enjoying the walk is perhaps not the person undertaking it. Could it be that the walker's body is in the *'service'* of another's mind? This may well be the meaning behind the phrase *'Every man jack wants to be what he is not.'* Certainly the sentence *'I've got a witch on my left shoulder'* suggests the walker is not in control of his body.

In H.G.Wells's 1911 story 'The Story of The Late Mr Elvesham', an ailing elderly philosopher swaps minds with a healthy youth. Whilst the older man enjoys a new lease of life, the youth finds himself trapped in a failing body. It seems possible that in 'Service' a young man's mind is experiencing a walk in the body of an elderly man.

KEY LINE: *'Why do you have a cloud in your eye?'*

'The Ballard of J. Drummer'

The narrator informs us this tale is set in the year 199601, before adding *'The last numeral was upside down.'* This text was in fact written in the year 1996, so the addition of the 01 could indicate that the events take place in an alternate or supplemental version of the present.

He relates how a musician, by the name of Johnny Drummer, arrives on the outskirts of a town only to be met with anger and rejection from the townsfolk. For this is an age when drum programming and computer generated rhythms have come to dominate.

The line *'Two sticks make up a cross'* serves a double purpose. It signifies that being a drummer is the musician's cross to bear. But it is also suggestive of a crucifix that can be used to ward off vampires. After all, the events seem to play out like a mix of western and horror story. The tale even concludes with a moral: *'Don't ever follow the path of being hard and tough when your heart is soft.'*

It's worth pointing out that rather than a 'Ballad' this is styled as a 'Ballard' – as in the sci-fi author J.G. Ballard, whose books Mark had read as a young man. Is it stretching things too far to think Mark may have viewed the story of a manual musician out of his depth in a digital world as a contender for one of Ballard's *Myths of the Near Future*?

KEY LINE: *'He looked into the mirror and said "I am not him".'*

'Hurricane Edward'

A farm hand in Ross County (possibly a reference to the county of the same name in the Scottish Highlands) recounts the story of how a hurricane devastated the farm. A certain Mr Hughes, who is most probably the farm's owner, had predicted the hurricane, because *'He knew this climate.'*

It's hard to read this text and not be reminded of the shattering thunderstorm recounted in H.P. Lovecraft's 1923 story 'The Lurking Fear'. Indeed, the supernatural is present here also, as, in an unexpected twist, it's revealed that due to his unpreparedness, the farm hand in fact died during the hurricane. Consequently, the story is being related from beyond the grave.

It seems the farm hand has only recently passed over into the spirit world, and is still grappling with his new state. *'I'm not an ordinary guy. Am I?'* he asks. He goes on to recall the familiar details of his life before the hurricane came: *'Asleep at twelve thirty in cosy cots'*. But there is a sense of forced nostalgia, a sense that he is according the memories more warmth than they deserve.

Elsewhere the line *'I held yellow thick ropes'* has the vibrancy and economy of the prose of Stephen King. It should also be noted that Mark's middle name is Edward – and that the hurricane is referred to as *'he.'* So might Mark therefore be acknowledging his reputation as an unpredictable and destructive force?

KEY LINE: *'There are characters in my brain.'*

THE 2000S

'Dr. Bucks' Letter'

The story opens up with a Mr J. McCarthy reflecting on how a previously *'hard won friendship'* has been deeply damaged by his own actions. He recalls how he lost his temper, mocked his friend *'and treated him with rudeness'*.

Whilst he hopes they may be able to reconnect in the future, the current loss of the friendship is causing him to sink into depression. Matters are compounded when he receives a letter from a certain Doctor Bucks, regarding his welfare benefits.

He decides to cheer himself up by listening to the radio and reading a magazine. He happens upon an article entitled 'The Essence of Tong' that he reads out loud. The article is written by a second narrator who details the unremarkable assortment of things he never leaves home without: *'Cassettes, CDs, palm pilot'* etc. Strangely, when the article is over, we never return to the 'real world' of the original narrator. He simply remarks *'I was in the realm of The Essence of Tong.'*

What makes this especially curious is the article in question is a real interview with DJ Pete Tong, taken from the Virgin Trains free magazine *HotLine*. With its blending of the fictional and the factually banal, 'Dr. Bucks' Letter' has the atmosphere and atypical structure of one of J.G. Ballard's experimental short stories of the early 1980s.

KEY LINE: *'Of my own making, I walk a dark corridor of my heart.'*

'Last Commands of Xyralothep Via MES'

The name Xyralothep is undoubtedly inspired by the strange being Nyarlathotep, who features in a number of H.P. Lovecraft's stories. Also known as The Crawling Chaos, Nyarlathotep is a grotesque and malign deity. In contrast, the commands of Xyralothep, whilst occasionally brash and harsh, would seem to largely consist of sound advice.

In the lyric, Mark addresses Xyralothep with the words *'This is your vessel MES.'* Although the language here feels carefully assembled, there seems to be an acknowledgement that Mark sometimes acts as a conduit for ideas from the ether.

This is not a narrative in the strictest sense, yet the notion of a human being used as a vessel to transmit commands from a creature from another dimension is well within the gothic tradition. We are also given just enough information to be able to summon up a sense of a specific world.

The commands are being transmitted by Mark, whilst he is in the fictional town of Speck Marsden. The name is possibly inspired by one of a number of English towns called Marsden. But perhaps this is 'spec Marsden' as in a speculative version of a town. Once again the story doesn't operate in a discreet world. Mark reminds us that it is but part of a wider reality: *'Mountain's waters blocked by dormant tree – see later on this LP'*.

KEY LINE: *'Deploreth thy real god.'*

'Blindness'

There are a few different iterations of the lyrics to 'Blindness', but the most rewarding set are the ones recorded for the version of the song on the group's final John Peel session in 2004. The fact the recording in question is one of the group's finest of the era makes for a doubly satisfying experience.

The story the narrator recounts sounds not so much like a dream, more like a fugue or something experienced whilst in a heightened state. The line *'I was talking to Jane Seymour, eyes wide open, the neck was slightly dislocated'* immediately grabs the attention. The likely assumption is that the protagonist is in conversation with British actress Jane Seymour. Yet, the reference to the neck summons thoughts of Henry the VIII's third wife. However, Seymour died of post-natal complications rather than beheading. Maybe this is why the neck was only *'slightly dislocated.'* From there, the song evolves via a series of sightings of posters in central Manchester that seem to herald the appearance of a frightening blind man.

Mark claimed in an interview, that 'Blindness' concerned the blind Labour Party MP David Blunkett, who was at that point the Home Secretary. Blunkett's hardline policies had clearly positioned him as an opponent of civil liberties, hence the references to curfews and posters saying '*Do you work hard?*'

But there is far more going on here than a simple critique of an unpopular MP. The line *'I was only on one leg'* could well refer to masonic initiation rites. Initiates are also blindfolded, so they experience temporary blindness.

The reference to Jane Seymour may actually allude to the actress's best-known role, in the 1973 James Bond film *Live and Let Die*, in which she plays Solitaire: a girl with a gift for tarot readings. The tarot, like freemasonry, has its roots in the early Egyptian Mystery Schools, which are believed to have imparted secret knowledge from ancient times.

On a more prosaic level, *'I was only on one leg'* may also refer to an incident that occurred a few months before 'Blindness' received its debut: Mark slipped on some ice, breaking his hip and leg, leading to him undertaking several Fall gigs in a wheelchair.

KEY LINE: *'I said, "Blind man, have mercy on me!"'*

'What About Us?'

Is this the story of serial killer Doctor Harold Shipman, as seen through the eyes of a rabbit? Nothing nearly so simple it would seem. Whilst the story begins in earnest with the lines *'I am a rabbit from East Germany, I was very happy'* Mark has denied that the song is from the perspective of an actual animal. In fact, he stated during an interview that the text concerned an East German drug dealer.

Despite this claim, it shouldn't go unremarked that Mark and his wife Elena owned a toy rabbit they named Gunther, which was purchased in Germany. The pair used to weave jokes and stories around Gunther, so it's not impossible that the narrative is actually being seen from the perspective of a toy.

From East Germany the dealer/rabbit/toy moves to the North of England, where he feels a great sense of disappointment. Then, by a refuse bin, he happens upon a newspaper article that describes the crimes of Dr Harold Shipman. This is a different kind of drug dealer, one who deals out death. Shipman was a Yorkshire GP who is believed to have murdered up to 260 of his patients, by injecting them with lethal doses of painkillers.

Shipman had hung himself whilst in his prison cell on January 13th 2004, just six months before the song's first appearance at a Fall gig.

KEY LINE: *'I saw a newspaper, I was not very happy.'*

'Is This New'

Written for the album *Imperial Wax Solvent*, the text opens up with the narrator trying to recall on which daytime television show he saw a certain Mr J. Archer (who may possibly be the best selling author and disgraced Conservative MP Jeffrey Archer). *'It was something like Judge and jury, or Jeremy Kyle.'*

The narrator reports that Archer *'separated everywhere'*, which might be a reference to a breakdown or schizophrenia, or possibly to Archer having become splintered through time. The TV show manages to identify the man's mother Dot and his friend Judy (TV presenter Judy Finnigan?), but nevertheless they keep searching – possibly for the multiple versions of Archer.

The repeated references to *'Time Blenders'* tends to support the idea that what we are being presented with is much more than just a comment on the questionable value of daytime TV. Instead, it's a vision with elements of both science fiction and Kafkaesque mystery. This is especially noticeable in the reference to *'The last statement with the department of no name.'*

To increase the sense of labyrinthine machinations 'the department of no name' is also mentioned in the text for 'Alton Towers' that appears on the same album.

KEY LINE: *'It was not in accord with any known law!'*

THE 2010S

'O.F.Y.C. Showcase'

This piece is taken from the *Your Future Our Clutter* album – a release that saw Mark creating an even greater interconnectivity between the lyrics of several different compositions.

The scene would seem to be at least partly set somewhere away from the UK. The narrator observes (possibly from the vantage point of a tobacco kiosk: *'little 'baco mongers'*) a parade of ex-pats with archaic names like *'Archibald'* and *'Old Yates'*. Initially it seems possible this is a vision from the past, but as events unfold it appears we are in the present.

It's probable that Mark is talking from a personal perspective here. The reference to making the land *'a showcase of Fall talent'* suggests he may well be scanning these ex-pats for potential future group members.

The line *'There goes Austin down, completes what's going down, back and around ink you lot'* almost certainly refers to the writer Austin Collings who had recently co-written Mark's autobiography *Renegade: The Lives and Tales of Mark E. Smith.*

KEY LINE: *'There goes that yankee, who gets ex-pats to go on Quality Street.'*

'Nate Will Not Return'

This is perhaps the most fervent example of Mark's 'clang process', with the majority of the lyric being fuelled by rhyming assonance. The action is primarily focussed on an actor called Nate, who visits London and, during a telephone call with his father, reflects on his ambitions and concerns. As noted elsewhere, the title is almost certainly corrupted from the *Twilight Zone* episode 'King 9 Will Not Return'.

As is often the case with Mark's texts, it's the sudden magnification of detail that takes you by surprise. Here, it's the moment we suddenly zero in on a Russian maid, working in New York as an illegal immigrant, who, due to her overtime, is unable to watch *Gossip Girl* – a US romantic TV drama aimed at teens.

It should also be mentioned that *Gossip Girl* features a character called Nate Archibald, played by the handsome Chace Crawford. So the song's title could refer to the character of Nate being written out of the TV drama. Either way, the narrative's perspective appears to slide between Nate as actor and Nate as character. It's also possible that he is the same Archibald referred to in 'O.F.Y.C. Showcase'.

KEY LINE: *'I perchance do decide to replicate.'*

'Loadstones'

The narrator informs us *'And after dark sunset, my brother and I, we walked the path, far from the tower.'* Once again we are in the realm of gothic horror. We know Mark isn't speaking from his own perspective here, as in reality he has three sisters but no brothers.

This is another fragmented tale, told through sharp snapshot images. The entire text is veiled in an atmosphere of uncertainty and unease, wherein the author pares down the information to its most essential elements.

As ever, there are several specific details that catch the attention. The image of *'shoes for the dead'* for instance. Or the use of *'Island of Wight'*, as opposed to the usual Isle of Wight. Whilst the phrase *'the pill police'* feels like a visitation from another kind of story altogether.

A lodestone is a naturally magnetised piece of mineral, with the ability to attract iron. Perhaps it is this very power which asserts such a strong effect on the characters' blood. Lodestones were also used as the very first magnetic compasses – the Old English word 'lode' meaning 'journey, or way'.

Yet Mark chooses to spell it loadstones. This may be an affectation, but it's quite possibly intended to imply the loadstones are a burden to be borne. Perhaps the loadstones are an oppressive and negative influence on *'the parish'* – like the standing stones in the 1977 children's supernatural TV drama *Children of the Stones.*

KEY LINE: *'A light sea breeze ruffles blood, skin is bleeding.'*

'First One Today'

Mark described the lyric as "social commentary", and its subject matter would seem to be familiar enough. The protagonist is caught up in the process of endlessly documenting the boring minutiae of his life, by taking photographs with his smart phone.

He's also engaged in other activities that mark him out as a bland, modern man, such as entering a bar and ordering a *'New Coke Latte.'* There is fortunately no such drink. However, like Philip K. Dick, Mark was fond of inventing fictional products, services and organisations that *sound* as if they belong in the real world.

Further examples include Fibre Book, The Birmingham School of Business School, The Broken Brother Pentacle Church, Hotel Amnesia, *The Vitamin B Glandular Show*, and a new programme called *The Kettisons.*

There are other details in the text of 'First One Today' that imply the situation is far more off-kilter than its subject matter would initially suggest. The repeated references to shootings hint that the taking of a photo is a potentially aggressive act. Indeed, an alternate reading of the narrative is that the 'shootings' are actual murders. If so, then the killer seems to be extremely indiscriminate and dispassionate, shooting a waitress even as he pays for his coffee.

If Mark's earlier work often bore the influence of *The Twilight Zone* or *Night Gallery*, then 'First One Today' seems to surf the same zeitgeist as Charlie Brooker's dark anthology series *Black Mirror.*

KEY LINE: *'There stands the door, within, a man.'*

'Couples vs Jobless Mid 30s'

Written for the final Fall album *New Facts Emerge*, 'Couples vs Jobless Mid 30s' is a lengthy composition, representing Mark at his most fervently Burroughsian.

A series of short cryptic phrases and words accumulate to create a mosaic of desperation. In contrast, the title appears to mock catchpenny film titles such as *Cowboys vs. Aliens* (2011) and *Cockneys vs. Zombies* (2012). But, within this specific scenario, the conflict is largely between a young man still living at home, and the mother who repeatedly shouts at him to *'get a job!'*

Or perhaps the title refers back to 1979's 'Spectre vs. Rector'. For there are several intimations of the gothic here too, with references to *'gargoyles'* and an *'elf grin'*, not to mention the line *'His blonde mother spouse tortures him in his big house.'*

Meanwhile, the use of the phrase *'No, nevermore'* inevitably summons up thoughts of Edgar Allan Poe – just as it did when Mark deployed it in the 1984 text for 'Elves'. Another lyrical quote buried in mix is the chorus from Jacques Brel's 1962 song 'Les Bourgeois', including the line *'les bourgeois c'est comme les cochons'*, which translates as *'the bourgeois are like pigs.'*

Despite being one of Mark's very last compositions, 'Couples vs Jobless Mid 30s' still displays his desire to experiment and blend seemingly disparate sources, and it contains turns of phrase that can rank amongst his best work, including the sinister *'awkwardly descend to great terror'* and the unforgettable reference to *'clotted breath.'*

KEY LINE: *'He implodes on shelf, with someone else.'*

▲ ▲ ▲

SEE ALSO

Mark E. Smith – *The Post Nearly Man* (1998)

A spoken word album unlike any other you'll hear, and definitely not one for the faint of heart. A mix of studio recordings and lo-fi dictaphone fragments, this is a deeply experimental collection featuring plenty of rough edged tape collage. The closest analogue is probably William S. Burroughs's tape cut-ups album *Nothing Here Now But the Recordings* (1981).

As ever, Mark is keen to confound expectations, so not only does his spoken word album include music, it also features readings from other voices besides his own. Despite having the space to create more expansive narratives – such as the ten minutes plus of the menacing multi-voiced thriller 'Visit of an American Poet' – he chooses to keep his texts as abstracted and splintered as ever.

Also, as befits all the best Fall LPs, there's even a cover version; the album opens with Mark and others reading/performing an adaptation of 'The Horror in Clay', the opening chapter of Lovecraft's classic short story 'The Call of Cthulhu'.

No Place Like It (1999)

This is a short story written by Mark, and published in Penguin's *City Life Book of Manchester Short Stories*. Three disgruntled men meet and decide to form a political party, although it's unclear what their aims are.

It opens with a hefty, paragraph-long sentence that snares the attention with phrases like '*the gross arrogance, blatant incompetence and thievery of the white trash*.' The two and a quarter page story also rather cheekily includes a reference to a pub called *Finnegan's Wake*.

Pander! Panda! Panzer!
(2002)

A spoken word album unlike any other you'll hear. Unless you've already heard *The Post Nearly Man*. This second collection of stories, 'poems' and incantations sees Mark experimenting further with text and sound collage. The album is edited together as one continuous piece, and whilst there's a slightly more cohesive feel to the whole enterprise, it simultaneously sounds even more intangible.

Highlights include the murky, hypnotic 'Who Are We And How Did We Get There?' and a section where Mark and his wife Elena Poulou read excerpts from one of Mark's film synopses.

▲ ▲ ▲

FURTHER RESOURCES

If you have the inclination, but more importantly the time, I can recommend no finer resources than the following.

The Annotated Fall
http://annotatedfall.doomby.com/

For those with a special interest in Mark's words, this is the site for you. Every Fall lyric, with annotations harvested from a variety of sources. It's full of well-researched references and background detail, alongside learned observations, healthy speculation and wild theories. Plus a lively, informative comments section that constantly adds to the vast resource of information therein.

The Fall Online
https://thefall.org/

This is the largest resource of Fall related information on the web; more than enough to entertain both new fans and old. Including detailed discography, gigography, bibliography, lyrics and a photographic archive. There are also multiple first hand reports of hundreds of gigs, plus set lists and more.

Fall Tracks A-Z
https://sites.google.com/site/reformationposttpm/fall-tracks

For those fascinated by recording and performance dates etc. herein you will encounter a mind-bending amount of factual information. Includes details on the various versions of any given song and its appearances on albums, singles, bootlegs, radio sessions and so on, as well as dates of the song's first and final performances.

▲ ▲ ▲

CTP Template: CD_INL3
Compact Disc Inside Inlay
Customer
Catalogue No.
Job Title
COLOURS
CYAN
MAGENTA
BLACK
Young Lovers;
ays Kill Them Both
DANGER
He Didn't Fake the Sna
SONG POEMS
ROCK
TERRIFIC $1.00
MYSTERIES
en sphinx
all kings

Dear Graham. SAT-OKT. 15'

Here's hoping you O.K. Didn't go Brazil, feet swelled up, no visas etc. Guitarist wants maternity leave, wife crackers – need the steel of you – Mark Search

WE MUST FIGHT the sneering part-time culturists of "ROYAL"-"EX" And 'SALFORD' RUE de Radclife – Riley-Wiley:

AND DESTROY Their 31st OCT. OPENING.

Anyway, ignore above – 20TH NOV, definitely on all well – you must help! Home/tour etc. Have 3-piece lesbian group – Massive good –

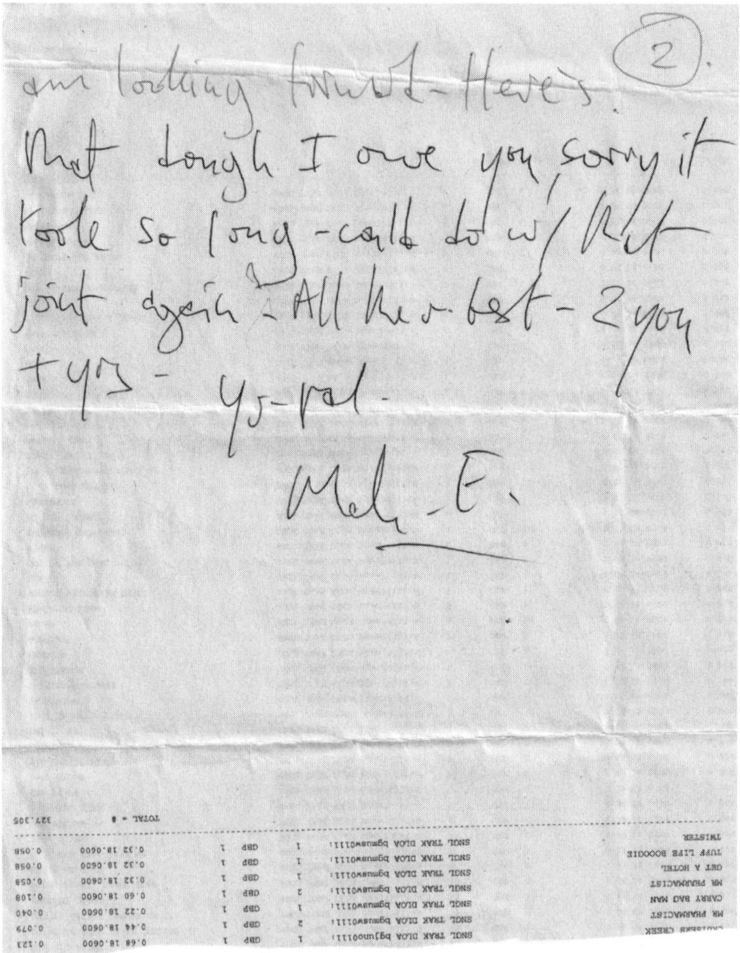

(2).

am looking forward – Here's
that dough I owe you, sorry it
took so long – can't do w/ that
joint again – All the v. best – 2 you
+ yrs – Yrs – Mark –

Mark E.

CRUISERS CREEK	SNGL TRAK DLOA bgjuno0111!	1	GBP	1	0.68 18.0600	0.123
MR PHARMACIST	SNGL TRAK DLOA bgmusw0111!	2	GBP	1	0.44 18.0600	0.079
CARRY BAG MAN	SNGL TRAK DLOA bgmusw0111!	1	GBP	1	0.22 18.0600	0.040
MR PHARMACIST	SNGL TRAK DLOA bgmusw0111!	2	GBP	1	0.60 18.0600	0.108
GET A HOTEL	SNGL TRAK DLOA bgmusw0111!	1	GBP	1	0.32 18.0600	0.058
TUFF LIFE BOOOGIE	SNGL TRAK DLOA bgmusw0111!	1	GBP	1	0.32 18.0600	0.058
TWISTER	SNGL TRAK DLOA bgmusw0111!	1	GBP	1	0.32 18.0600	0.058

TOTAL - $ 127.305

NEW BIG PRINZ	SNGL TRAK DLOA bgwe70111:W	[illegible]	[illegible]	[illegible]			
OVERTURE FROM 'I AM CURIOUS. O	SNGL TRAK DLOA bgwe70111:W	15	GBP	1	0.06	18.0600	0.011
DOG IS LIFE / JERUSALEM	SNGL TRAK DLOA bgwe70111:W	13	GBP	1	0.05	18.0600	0.009
KURIOUS ORANJ	SNGL TRAK DLOA bgwe70111:W	15	GBP	1	0.06	18.0600	0.011
WRONG PLACE. RIGHT TIME	SNGL TRAK DLOA bgwe70111:W	12	GBP	1	0.05	18.0600	0.009
GUIDE ME SOFT	SNGL TRAK DLOA bgwe70111:W	8	GBP	1	0.03	18.0600	0.005
C.D. WIN FALL 2088 AD	SNGL TRAK DLOA bgwe70111:W	8	GBP	1	0.03	18.0600	0.005
YES. O YES	SNGL TRAK DLOA bgwe70111:W	7	GBP	1	0.03	18.0600	0.005
VAN PLAGUE ?	SNGL TRAK DLOA bgwe70111:W	6	GBP	1	0.02	18.0600	0.004
BAD NEWS GIRL	SNGL TRAK DLOA bgwe70111:W	4	GBP	1	0.02	18.0600	0.004
CAB IT UP !	SNGL TRAK DLOA bgwe70111:W	5	GBP	1	0.02	18.0600	0.004
LAST NACHT	SNGL TRAK DLOA bgwe70111:W	5	GBP	1	0.02	18.0600	0.004
BIG NEW PRIEST	SNGL TRAK DLOA bgwe70111:W	5	GBP	1	0.02	18.0600	0.004
BAD NEWS GIRL	SNGL TRAK DLOA bgwe70111:W	1	GBP	1	0.00	18.0600	0.000
CAB IT UP !	SNGL TRAK DLOA bgwe70111:W	1	GBP	1	0.00	18.0600	0.000
LAST NACHT	SNGL TRAK DLOA bgwe70111:W	1	GBP	1	0.00	18.0600	0.000
PAINTWORK	SNGL TRAK DLOA bgwe70111:W	2	GBP	1	0.01	18.0600	0.002
I AM DAMO SUZUKI	SNGL TRAK DLOA bgwe70111:W	1	GBP	1	0.00	18.0600	0.000
VAN PLAGUE ?	SNGL TRAK DLOA bgwe70111:W	1	GBP	1	0.00	18.0600	0.000
MANSION	SNGL TRAK DLOA bgwe70111:W	1	GBP	1	0.00	18.0600	0.000
BOMBAST	SNGL TRAK DLOA bgwe70111:W	1	GBP	1	0.00	18.0600	0.000
BARMY	SNGL TRAK DLOA bgwe70111:W	1	GBP	1	0.00	18.0600	0.000
WHAT YOU NEED	SNGL TRAK DLOA bgwe70111:W	1	GBP	1	0.00	18.0600	0.000
SPOILT VICTORIAN CHILD	SNGL TRAK DLOA bgwe70111:W	1	GBP	1	0.00	18.0600	0.000
L.A.	SNGL TRAK DLOA bgwe70111:W	1	GBP	1	0.00	18.0600	0.000
GUT OF THE QUANTIFIER	SNGL TRAK DLOA bgwe70111:W	1	GBP	1	0.00	18.0600	0.000
VIXEN	SNGL TRAK DLOA bgwe70111:W	1	GBP	1	0.00	18.0600	0.000
COULDN'T GET AHEAD	SNGL TRAK DLOA bgwe70111:W	1	GBP	1	0.00	18.0600	0.000
MY NEW HOUSE	SNGL TRAK DLOA bgwe70111:W	1	GBP	1	0.00	18.0600	0.000
PAINTWORK	SNGL TRAK DLOA bgwe70111:W	1	GBP	1	0.00	18.0600	0.000
I AM DAMO SUZUKI	SNGL TRAK DLOA bgwe70111:W	1	GBP	1	0.00	18.0600	0.000
TO NK ROACHMENT: YARBLES	SNGL TRAK DLOA bgwe70111:W	1	GBP	1	0.00	18.0600	0.000
PETTY (THIEF) LOUT	SNGL TRAK DLOA bgwe70111:W	1	GBP	1	0.00	18.0600	0.000
ROLLIN' DANY	SNGL TRAK DLOA bgwe70111:W	1	GBP	1	0.00	18.0600	0.000
CRUISERS CREEK	SNGL TRAK DLOA bgwe70111:W	1	GBP	1	0.00	18.0600	0.000
MY NEW HOUSE	SNGL TRAK DLOA bgwe70111:W	1	GBP	1	0.00	18.0600	0.000
GROSS CHAPEL - BRITISH GRENADI	SNGL TRAK DLOA bgwe70111:W	1	GBP	1	0.00	18.0600	0.000
MANSION	SNGL TRAK DLOA bgwe70111:W	1	GBP	1	0.00	18.0600	0.000
BOMBAST	SNGL TRAK DLOA bgwe70111:W	1	GBP	1	0.00	18.0600	0.000
BARMY	SNGL TRAK DLOA bgwe70111:W	1	GBP	1	0.00	18.0600	0.000
WHAT YOU NEED	SNGL TRAK DLOA bgwe70111:W	1	GBP	1	0.00	18.0600	0.000
SPOILT VICTORIAN CHILD	SNGL TRAK DLOA bgwe70111:W	2	GBP	1	0.01	18.0600	0.002
L.A.	SNGL TRAK DLOA bgwe70111:W	2	GBP	1	0.01	18.0600	0.002
GUT OF THE QUANTIFIER	SNGL TRAK DLOA bgwe70111:W	2	GBP	1	0.01	18.0600	0.002
VIXEN	SNGL TRAK DLOA bgwe70111:W	2	GBP	1	0.01	18.0600	0.002
COULDN'T GET AHEAD	SNGL TRAK DLOA bgwe70111:W	2	GBP	1	0.01	18.0600	0.002
MY NEW HOUSE	SNGL TRAK DLOA bgwe70111:W	2	GBP	1	0.01	18.0600	0.002
PAINTWORK	SNGL TRAK DLOA bgwe70111:W	2	GBP	1	0.01	18.0600	0.002
LIVING TOO LATE	SNGL TRAK DLOA bgwe70111:W	1	GBP	1	0.00	18.0600	0.000
MR PHARMACIST	SNGL TRAK DLOA bgava20111:	1	GBP	1	5.28	18.0600	0.954

SUBTOTAL C/FWD = 326.57

MY FAVOURITE WHILE

Conversations with M.E.S.

On various occasions over the years, when Mark and I were brainstorming on either the anthology series ideas or working on plots for the film script, we would record these sessions on my iPhone. Inevitably however, our discussions would often veer onto other subjects.

Mark was a witty and vivid conversationalist, and for forty years, his interviews in the music press were unfailingly entertaining. So much so, they would be avidly read by many who would never dream of listening to The Fall's music. Mark could be insightful, perverse, contradictory and deliberately controversial. Like Spike Milligan, he was a deeply unpredictable interviewee who could never *ever* be considered a safe bet.

Despite this, it's worth noting that, his reputation as an authentic working class autodidact notwithstanding, Mark was also an astute showman. Therefore part of what he was doing in interviews was putting on a show: marking out his territory: projecting an image: defining the parameters of his persona. By way of contrast, the following exchanges are not interviews; rather they are conversations. That's part of what I think makes them interesting. There's a thoughtfulness and honesty here.

Naturally enough, our conversations regularly drifted onto our favourite films, favourite music and so on. After all, although Mark was a widely recognised artist, he would always remain a fan, and a shared love of the music of Can, and the films of Lindsay Anderson shine out of these exchanges.

Mark was also a very engaging storyteller, with a wonderful sense of the macabre. Witness the tale of his late night arrival at Sigmund Freud's house whilst speeding, or the description of an afternoon train journey from Manchester to Clitheroe, which he manages to imbue with the morbid, clammy dread of an M.R. James story.

Of course some of the time we're just riffing and trying to make each other laugh. Mark's sense of humour was as refined as it was daft and he would often reduce friends to fits of giggles with his rants and one-liners. Over my career as a writer I have been fortunate to work with some of the funniest men and women in the comedy business. But no one has made me laugh as much as Mark.

▲ ▲ ▲

I

JAMES JOYCE, LINDSAY ANDERSON & PRESTWICH MENTAL HOSPITAL

MARK: I did this thing a while back, for the bleedin' James Joyce Society.

GRAHAM: Did you set them straight?

(Laughter)

MARK: Yeah, I think I did, yeah.

GRAHAM: I know this is heresy, but I've never really been able to get into Joyce.

MARK: No, I think he is very good actually. Some of it, y'know. But this thing, it was *weird.* I was ready to leave and they fuckin'... They locked the door and showed this film. It was... it was not right, y'know what I'm saying?

GRAHAM: What?

MARK: Some art thing: worse thing you've ever seen in your life. It was like in fuckin'... y'know in *O Lucky Man!* where everywhere he goes he ends up being shown films. It was like that.

GRAHAM: What because...?

MARK: Soon as it started I knew why they'd locked the fuckin' door. Nobody would want to sit through that!

(Laughter)

GRAHAM: I watched *O Lucky Man!* again the week before last. Reckon that'd be about my 20th viewing.

MARK: Seriously?

GRAHAM: Thereabouts. I tell you though, even now I'm still seeing new things in it.

MARK: Oh it is fantastic. Yeah, I must've seen it at least five times meself. Lindsay Anderson was... he was fuckin' acidic! The best. If you want to know what Britain was like in 1973, watch *O Lucky Man!*

GRAHAM: Exactly! It's all there: every layer of society.

MARK: The more you think about it... It's superb. Actually I watched *Britannia Hospital* again a while back. It was a blow out watching it again. It is fuckin' fantastic.

GRAHAM: In terms of the storytelling in that, David Sherwin's writing is so strong. Things like... How he kills off the hero half way through the film, then brings him back as a 'monster'. It's amazing.

MARK: It's everything that films try to be now. And *O Lucky Man!* the more you watch it, you're right, the more there is in there. It's like Shakespeare or summat. The only thing is, I used to hate all that Alan Price music.

GRAHAM: Yeah well, to be honest, I've watched the film so many times now that I just love the music. It's so completely bound up in the film for me.

MARK: Yeah, yeah... That stuff with Alan Price and the band in the van and all that is quite interesting. And there's those great sections in it, where it has '4: The North of England'. And actually it is... when I was... funnily enough, in a way it's odd. But I was sort of...

I grew up with it. So *If....* when *If....* came out I was in the second year at grammar school. So I identified with it.

But then I'd never seen *O Lucky Man!* for years. But it was the same sort of thing. Like when it had '6: Yorkshire'. And at that time I was a shipping clerk, and every time I used to have to go to Yorkshire. And every time it was like a totally different world. And it shows that. He has to go into a strip club, to talk to the Mayor about getting a deal in Wakefield or summat. And that's what Yorkshire used to be like.

I used to go over on me motorbike from Salford docks, to talk to the guy, and you end up in a porn party. When I was about 17. In fuckin' Yorkshire, where I'd never been in me bleedin' life, on a motorbike, to get the guy to sign these import and export forms and I had to go in this club. And they had these strippers on, and the Mayor was in there, and I'm tryin' to get the guy to sign these forms.

And then in Lancashire at one point, a similar thing, I had to go to this bloke's house, and there's all these birds, and the fuckin' Mayor! Another Mayor! He didn't have any underpants on and he had a big fuckin' joint in his fuckin' hand!

(Laughter)

MARK: Ask Lynden! In the 70s! So the stories I tell people from the fuckin' 70s, nobody believes them. But they were things that happened to Malcolm McDowell, and they happened to *me*. I never noticed that to start. But it shook me up a bit watching it.

GRAHAM: I've watched it such a lot over the years. And it's always felt very contemporary really. But then, a couple of years ago, I was watching it at a screening in London, and all of a sudden it looked like the past y'know. The images of the North suddenly looked like how it looked when I was a kid.

MARK: Me too, yeah.

GRAHAM: And the bit at the scientific installation where there's the explosion. And the fire engines arrived, and they suddenly looked like vintage cars! They've got the big wheels at the base of the ladder y'know.

MARK: It's a bit disturbing for a person of my age. It's like a video diary of the things you couldn't film in them days. So you've got to give him that. That's why they should preserve it. I mean that fuckin' *Britannia Hospital*, it's fuckin' amazing. I remember when Prestwich Hospital was like that.

When I left home, I lived in a flat opposite Prestwich Hospital with two mental nurses. But y'know, if I see one of them to work, which was once in a blue fuckin' moon, to the hospital. The start of *Britannia Hospital* – it's a regular scene there y'know: pickets, nurses, all about summat like the soup was off or summat, in the mental home! And the mental patients'd mix with them. *(Laughs)* And y'know, a lot of people seemed to think the mental patients were saner than the staff. I used to have them round me flat now and again y'know.

But you sort of forget about all that, it's just day-to-day life. But seeing *Britannia Hospital* brought it all back y'know. I mean it must look ridiculous now. But that was not an exaggeration of how things were.

These nurses, they'd have a bag, the psychologists and the mental nurses. All the nurses, and whatever the thing they were in Prestwich, they used to have these little Biba bags. Y'know, a Biba bag, like a woman's bag. All the nurses, they all had these bags. Even the guy who stoked coal in the basement, who I used to get my pot off, he had one, a Biba bag. And I said "Why have you all got Biba bags: these zippy bags?" And it was coz they'd all bring a sign to work.

GRAHAM: What, to protest with?

MARK: Yeah!

(Laughter)

MARK: Coz it was one of the things that you brought to work, y'know what I mean. Twenty Number Six y'know, ten Embassy, your make-up, and a Biba bag with a protest fuckin' sign! That is the truth! Coz they were all unionised y'know. Even the er, psychologist was in a union. Coz he was a right scrounger. He used to come 'round and scrounge his tea. And I was on the dole. What a cunt he was. He was in a union for psychologists. (...*indistinct*...) And he would be telling psychologists between here and fuckin' London what to do. They could have put it in *Britannia Hospital*. He's not exaggerating the truth y'know.

GRAHAM: Graham Crowden who plays Professor Millar...

MARK: He's fuckin' perfect! What an actor he is!

GRAHAM: I did three radio series with Graham. And the whole time I was saying to him "So Graham, on *O Lucky Man!*...".

(Laughter)

MARK: He was in sci-fi things wasn't he? He's such a good fuckin'... He *is* a consultant at Prestwich Hospital man, I'm tellin' yer. There were so many of them walking around y'know. He's just totally that role. I want to watch that again!

▲ ▲ ▲

2

CAN, HOUSE MUSIC & MARSHALL JEFFERSON'S DOG

MARK: Thanks for the CD by the way. That was great actually, because my copy of *Tago Mago* is fuckin'… It is scratched to fuck. But I couldn't go buy it myself, y'know.

GRAHAM: Why?

MARK: Well, y'know… I couldn't. Y'know what I'm saying?

GRAHAM: What, you couldn't be seen going into a record shop and buying a Can album?

MARK: No… it's not that…

GRAHAM: It's not like in the 70s, when the police treated it as a misdemeanour. It wouldn't end up on your permanent record.

(Laughter)

MARK: No, it's just y'know, it's hip to buy Can records nowadays. It is. See it all the time in Manchester.

GRAHAM: *Tago Mago* was the first Can album I ever heard.

MARK: Yeah me too. That was the first one I bought. Mail order. You couldn't fuckin' get it otherwise. I was into the Velvet Underground. But then Can! I tell you, when I was working on the docks, Can saved my life. That's what people don't understand now. Now it's *hip* to be into Can, you know what I'm sayin'? But y'see a lot of people want to say they like Can. But most of 'em, they don't really get what it is that's going on.

GRAHAM: It's still my favourite Can album. 'Mushroom' and 'Bring Me Coffee Or Tea'. It's like... You can just hear they're all bringing the best out of each other. The band is so tight.

MARK: Well that's what you fuckin' want isn't it? Yeah it's very... I was mad into Can. I learnt a lot from *Tago Mago*. I tell you the other one I played the most: *Soundtracks*. Have you heard that?

GRAHAM: Yeah. Brilliant. 'Tango Whiskyman'!

MARK: These films you've never seen 'em in your bleedin' life. But the music! What's that er... 'Don't Turn The Light On'? Jaki's fuckin' drumming on that!

GRAHAM: A mate of mine is a sound engineer. And about 20 years ago he worked with Holger Czukay. And he came into the studio one morning and apparently Holger had come in over night and dug out a huge hole in one of the studio walls so he could thread some piano wire through and twang it!

MARK: See a lot of people, they think Can is just fuckin' Holger. But it's fuckin' not. Even now, the Germans couldn't care less about Can.

GRAHAM: What else you listening to at the moment?

MARK: All sorts. Been listening to a lot of Italian house actually. They fuckin'... The sound... They have this very clear sound, you get me?

GRAHAM: What do you like about house, the repetition?

MARK: No, I like the whole thing, y'know.

GRAHAM: A lot of recent house is a bit too smooth for me.

MARK: Yeah, I know what you're saying, yeah.

GRAHAM: If you listen to early acid tunes, stuff like Adonis or Bam Bam or whatever, they've got a rough edge. They've got a… a wrongness. I mean Marshall's tunes are classic examples of that. They are perfect, but at the same time they sound a bit 'wrong'. And I love that.

MARK: Marshall is very good actually. People don't fuckin' realise how good he is.

GRAHAM: I still can't quite get my head around the fact Marshall Jefferson is living in Prestwich!

MARK: Hey, did I tell you about his walking machine?

GRAHAM: No.

MARK: Marshall's got this fuckin' dog right – this fuckin' thing! And he can't be arsed to walk it, so he bought a fuckin' exercise machine to walk the dog for him!

GRAHAM: Seriously?

MARK: Yeah. So he puts the dog on the fuckin' conveyer belt thing and he leaves him to it. And Marshall's goin' to me "Oh he loves it. He loves his walking machine." I said, "Yeah I bet he does. I bet he's much happier in your fuckin' bedroom than he would be running around the park chasing squirrels!"

▲ ▲ ▲

3

BEREAVEMENT & DREAMS

MARK: How's your Mum been coping since your Dad died?

GRAHAM: I think she's as okay as she can be to be honest. It's only been two months and it's her birthday today, so I'm sure that can't be easy. We were talking this morning and she said she still felt quite numb. I think we're *all* still taking it in really. But my Mum seems to be good at moving forward by treating everything as a series of tasks, if that makes sense.

MARK: Oh yeah, completely. My Mum was like General Patton!

(Laughter)

GRAHAM: I can imagine.

MARK: No she was actually. She was so organised it was unnerving.

(Laughter)

GRAHAM: There's no right or wrong way is there?

MARK: I still think about me Dad a lot y'know. It fuckin'… it doesn't go does it?

GRAHAM: Oh man, I had a dream with my Dad in, last week. First one since he died. It was just his voice. He called my name just before I woke up. When I was a teenager, my bedroom was up in the loft. He'd call my name, when it was mealtimes. It was like that. I woke up and I thought he'd called my name in the real world and it'd been him that woke me up. Then I remembered.

MARK: I go through fuckin' phases where I dream about me Dad all the time. And then… Yeah, not dreamt about him for… yeah a while.

GRAHAM: Do you still use ideas from dreams in songs?

MARK: Yeah I do actually: bits and pieces. Sometimes things… things just stick in your head from dreams, you understand me? I'm always looking.

GRAHAM: Have you seen *Inception*?

MARK: No. Any good?

GRAHAM: It's ok. It's not essential. The reason I mention it, is they play around with dreams. But in the end, it's one of those like *The Matrix*, where they turn a potentially fascinating idea into cops and robbers.

MARK: Is it one of them fuckin' *long* films?

GRAHAM: It is pretty long yeah, maybe two and a half hours. It could be shorter without any ill effects.

MARK: There's no need for it is there?

GRAHAM: I got a good character name from a dream. I was standing in a queue and there were these two middle-aged women in front of me and one of them said to the other "Do you know who I really like? Erk Finnan." So I used Erk Finnan for a character.

MARK: Erk Finnan! *(Laughs)* That is very good. What sort of character was he?

GRAHAM: It was in *Nebulous*. He was a very successful businessman. They called him 'The Danish back bacon baron'.

(Laughter)

MARK: I tell you… The names some people give their fuckin' kids nowadays, I reckon a lot of them must've come to 'em in fuckin' dreams! It's Yog-Sothoth putting 'em up to it!! Yeah!!! Yeah!!!

(Laughter)

▲ ▲ ▲

4

RICH PEOPLE & MANAGERS

MARK: Rich people, they used to have some kind of class about them didn't they? Y'know what I mean?

GRAHAM: Did they? I dunno.

MARK: No! Exactly.

(Laughter)

MARK: No, but there's a bigger discrepancy isn't there? Y'know, I've hung out with very *rich* people, and they're the meanest, most unhappy people. That's the sort of thing they do. I got in a fuckin'… what are them sports cars called?

GRAHAM: Porsche?

MARK: Porsche, yeah. Best Porsche. This fuckin' Dutchman who I used to know… Unbelievable y'know: I mean he fuckin' picked up this model bird. She dropped dead from ecstasy. He got away with it. Anyway, I remember going 'round to his house and he had every drawer full of every drug in the world, y'know. Marvellous feller. *(Laughs)* But he was so fuckin' filthy rich. His wife was Swiss. But y'know like, he gave me his fuckin' razor blade out of his fuckin' bag.

He's still got like Dutch credit… secret fuckin' Dutch fuckin' bank accounts y'know. Fuckin' lucky I must admit. Y'know for like five hundred deutsche er… y'know, gilders. He's had it renewed the week before, y'know what I mean? That tight! That's rich people. Then he goes out. He goes down to his Porsche, he's got about eight parkin' fines on his Porsche. Amounting to about four grand y'know what I mean? Just while we've been in his house waiting for his wife to come home.

And he's got, he's got this fuckin' bank. He's got this purse basically, stuffed with bits of post y'know. Y'know, like what I've got y'know – if you lose – with a tenner in it. But he's got ones with five thousand knicker in 'em, you know what I mean? It's like why? But that's what they're like, they're always paranoid that yer after it.

That'll be his taste, y'know what I mean? As a rich boy he's doing his duty. He must have been brought up like that. Watch the pennies and all this crap.

Oh we were talking about Bono weren't we? I can feel him through the waves... No, no urrgh! Their manager resigned. Oh fuckin' hell, that'll be crippling. Yeah, they'll be lost without him. He's a fuckin' smart fella. Very smart. He's the one Peter Grant nearly fuckin' laid out at the Haçienda. Peter Grant y'know, the Led Zeppelin manager?

GRAHAM: Yeah.

MARK: Coz he put forward a proposition with the simple Simply Red manager, that all fuckin' erm… musicians should sign over writing royalties, over to the managers of the groups. Y'know, bring it in as law an' all that. Unbelievable! The manager of U2 and er, Simply Red, all these people and these rock college people all sat there agreeing with 'em y'know. There's kids doing these sixth form…

And it went on like that. It was like a private… It was Simply Red's manager, fuckin' U2, Led Zep's manager Peter Grant, he did it a week before he died. And some other sinister cunt. And they were saying all groups – before anybody should be able to y'know, be a group – they have to sign… they had to get a manager, all this shit. Seriously touted that you have to get a manager and he's got to go to this managing school – and the manager gets all the royalties, all the gig money *(Laughs)*. Honestly, it's fuckin' preposterous.

But anyway, Peter Grant was there and he fuckin' grabbed him by the fuckin' neck – this U2 guy and the Simply Red guy – and he went "Listen you two pieces of fuckin' shit!" He said y'know, "You're not the reason we're in this business y'know." He went… What was the drummer's name in Led Zep?

GRAHAM: John Bonham.

MARK: He says "You're not the reason I'm in this business!! FUCKIN' JOHN BONHAM WAS THE REASON I WAS IN THIS FUCKIN' BUSINESS!!!" And banged their heads together! And fuckin' walked off.

(Laughter)

MARK: Brilliant that. I never liked Led Zep 'til then.

(Laughter)

MARK: But what a fuckin' manager! I said to Ed, "Can you fuckin' *do* that?" He said, "Er… er…" I said "Yeah, exactly!" It's the only way to deal with them isn't it? "John Bonham was why I was in this business". *They* were in the business… basically to rip young lads off. Under the pretence it's an intellectual sort of er… y'know what I mean?

"John Bonham was the fuckin' reason I got into this business!" Quite right. Fuckin'… You should, if you're gonna be a manager, you should love yer fuckin' mates shunt yer. First fuckin' rule. Never mind 'all the roadies can get the bus to rehearsals' and all this. There's all these rules they're making up. It's nothing to do with the manager what the group does really in a lot of ways!

▲ ▲ ▲

5

CLITHEROE, HEBDEN BRIDGE & BURNLEY

GRAHAM: So are you recording at the moment, or are you…?

MARK: Yeah, I've just done an EP yeah. That was a good idea. Fuckin'…

GRAHAM: And is that with everybody? Is that with Dave and…?

MARK: Yeah, we did it all separate because they're all on leave. The idea was to get an EP out right after the LP. So it's finally been done. It's good: different.

GRAHAM: Is it all new stuff or is it…?

MARK: Yeah, yeah, yeah. It's called *The Remainderer*. So everybody thinks it's stuff left over from the LP. It's not at all. Did it in Castleford. What a fuckin' joint that is. You could do a film in Castleford.

GRAHAM: Really? What sort of place?

MARK: Not Castleford. No sorry, Clitheroe!

GRAHAM: Oh Clitheroe. Yeah, I've got a sister who lives in Clitheroe.

MARK: Yeah?

GRAHAM: We were talking about Clitheroe today, it's a weird place.

There's a lot of fucking money in Clitheroe now. A lot of very wealthy people there.

MARK: I know. Coz that is an episode in itself man. It is an episode. The recording of The Fall EP is an episode. We could start off like that. The recording of the new Fall LP.

GRAHAM: I think it'd be great to have something like that – the haunted studio idea – and then a few other more ambiguous ideas around it. Clitheroe now is like sort of Hale or Alderley Edge.

MARK: I know.

GRAHAM: Women in make-up you would have only ever seen women wear at night time, out to the butchers in fur coats. Like footballer's wives y'know.

MARK: I know Hebden Bridge is like that.

GRAHAM: Yeah, Hebden Bridge is like hippie fall-out, but then the next generation.

MARK: Good for them y'know. But I keep boring the lads about it: Hebden Bridge. I used to deal acid out at fuckin' Hebden Bridge. I tell you, in about 1975, I used to deal acid there and get grass. I remember this fuckin' hippie, he was fuckin' going for Mayor. He was going for Mayor in Hebden Bridge, but he didn't even wear any trousers or anything like that.

(Laughter)

MARK: He said if you want to get down with us in Hebden Bridge – in Haslingdon he could get you two houses for four hundred and fifty quid.

GRAHAM: Fuck.

MARK: And fuckin' one in bloody Hebden Bridge, for fifteen hundred knicker. And this insurance salesman from Australia, he were one of me best mates at the time, he said we could do it right. And I could have done it then. If I'd have done that, if I could have cobbled together two grand, I could have had two houses in Haslingdon and one in fuckin' Hebden Bridge!

GRAHAM: Houses in Hebden Bridge are worth a fortune now.

MARK: I know. It's like two point… And I said to him, y'know "Fuckin' look, I'm not doin' it." Y'know, when you're 17!! He said, "I'm fuckin' doing you a big fuckin' deal, comin' up here. You will be… you will be sorry man." In his Aussie accent. I was like "Fuck off!"

GRAHAM: I'm not sure the ones in Haslingdon would…

MARK: Is Haslingdon not good?

GRAHAM: No, it's alright. It's not as flashy as Hebden Bridge!

MARK: Anyway, whatever.

GRAHAM: They reckon Burnley is the cheapest place for property. I don't know if it still is, but for a time, it was the suicide capitol of Europe.

MARK: Really?

GRAHAM: Yeah. It's brilliant that John Cooper Clarke stuff about the hotel in Burnley. What is it… *"It was a small room. I put the key in the lock and I broke the window."*

(Laughter)

MARK: *"I asked for a suite with a view and I got a Polo mint."*

(Laughter)

MARK: What I didn't know about Clitheroe, was how far away it was. For someone who's been everywhere...

GRAHAM: It's about an hour from here isn't it I suppose?

MARK: No it's not. That's one of the weird things. It's actually about as far as Liverpool from our house. You wouldn't think that. The last time I went to Clitheroe was like in 1983, to play a free concert at the castle. When it was all fuckin' stumbling salesmen in the rubble and weavers committing suicide, y'know what I mean? You go back to it now and it's...

GRAHAM: It's a bit gentrified isn't it?

MARK: I dunno, fuckin' hell, I wouldn't live there for all the money in China y'know.

GRAHAM: My sister's been living there for about two years.

MARK: Has she? The bass player lives there.

GRAHAM: Oh does he? Before that, she lived in Great Harwood. I don't know if you know Great Harwood.

MARK: Vaguely.

GRAHAM: It's between Accrington and Blackburn. It's just a little market town that hasn't had a market for probably about twenty odd years. That's where we grew up.

MARK: I mean imagine if you're in a studio. And even the bass player don't turn up – who lives in the fuckin' town – won't turn up for a session. There's summat up there isn't there? Y'know what I mean? This is a good sequence.

GRAHAM: I think the haunted studio is...

MARK: I've got all the out-takes.

GRAHAM: Deal me in.

MARK: It is very good. We could do a reconnaissance of it. It's all up there. Coz it was the EP, and it was doin' me fuckin' head in. It was just like fuckin' ridiculous. It's got to be done man. The more I think about, it's the Grand in Clitheroe. Do some research on the Grand in Clitheroe. We played the Grand in the dark. And they said y'know… Coz we didn't want to play Clitheroe, like on the tour for the last LP. So they said if we played they'd give us a week's free studio time.

GRAHAM: Oh really? Well, why not?

MARK: It's pitch black as we check in, so I thought 'oh right'. And we played there, so we took 'em up on their offer.

GRAHAM: So did you stay in Clitheroe, or did you 'commute'?

MARK: No I didn't stay in fuckin' Clitheroe!

(Laughter)

GRAHAM: Everybody I met in Clitheroe was pretty rude.

MARK: Very rude. Animalistic.

GRAHAM: It's like a principality! A feudal state!

MARK: Well Dave lives there. He keeps getting these blokes in pubs picking fights with him. They're all over familiar.

(Laughter)

MARK: We can set it in a different… This studio in fuckin' Clitheroe, the stories I could tell you. I go there on me own to do the vocals y'know. We got all this free time, but I couldn't get in there.

GRAHAM: What, in the actual studio?

MARK: Yeah, yeah, there's different times. We had this week and a half free time. So I go on me own, on the train. And I went through, and I didn't know all these towns. On the train from Victoria to Clitheroe, like there's one called something like Ingo and one called Trrunkakkkkk!

(Laughter)

GRAHAM: I tell you, I think the best one is just outside Blackburn. It's called Hall-i'-th'-Wood. Like Hall in the Wood.

MARK: Come on, it's pure *Twilight Zone*!

GRAHAM: I know: it's brilliant.

MARK: It's like (sings) *dat-du-der-dat-du-der! Mark Smith, in a white shirt gets in a taxi, from his house. Dut-du-der! To Piccadilly Train Station. Rush hour. Dat-der-der… Gets on the Clitheroe traaaaaain…*

GRAHAM: And everything goes dark.

MARK: It didn't get dark. It got brighter and brighter, and crowdeder and crowdeder. And they weren't, they weren't, they fuckin' weren't… It was six o'clock and they were *not* office workers! Where were they going? And they wouldn't get off the train.

Hey, there was this fuckin' woman on the train right and she was… The day before I got on with Elena. About 4 o'clock or summat, which was really nice. And I got on the fuckin' six o'clock late, like an idiot, the day after. It set off fuckin' virtually empty from Manchester. And it just filled up with the… Like these two rich kids sat next to me, and they sort of pushed me over, y'know what I mean like? Two lads: one was Asian and one was fuckin' white, and they were just like gettin' on me fuckin' nerves.

You think 'It'll be over soon' y'know. And then it just got like crowded, by all these school kids. It's like ten past six. And there was like farmer types getting on at three a go. Then, all these mentally ill people. And then they were all like talking in these codes y'know what I mean?

Twenty past six, then suddenly we're in Bolton North East or summat, and then a load of fuckin' yobbos get on who sit in the bicycle pit. They want to be tough. And like they're not even threatening, because they're so mentally feeble. D'yer understand me? There's about six of them and they're all about eight foot six. And they're so retarded. And it's like H.P. Lovecraft or something d'yer understand? It's a fuckin' nightmare.

And then this woman gets on with glasses. Her body all contorted. And she's like Rosemary West, but fat y'know, like this. And like there's all these fuckin' kids, and like none of them are giving her their seats. And she's obviously a crip'. This lad next to me, I says to him, "Just get up for the woman will you?" So he gets up and I says: "Sit down there love". And she says "You what?" You know you're in the hills right! I says "Sit down there love." And she says "Just you stop fuckin' harassing me!!"

GRAHAM: Like hillbillies.

MARK: But worse. Worrrrse!! Coz you look out the window, and you can't get out, coz them trains they're all sealed aren't they? And it's just trees flashing past. Wrrrrsssssss!!! Wrrrrsssssss!!! Wrrrrsssssss!!!

▲ ▲ ▲

6

"HE KILLED THESE S.S. MEN"

GRAHAM: *Blackburn* though…

MARK: It's peculiar isn't it? Blackburn. And Bolton as well.

GRAHAM: I don't really know Bolton so well. But Blackburn's always been rough.

MARK: Oh it has, yeah. I got attacked by a fuckin' train-load of fuckin' Blackburn fans once, on their way home from some... But yeah, they're fuckin' weird aren't they?

GRAHAM: When I was a kid, there was always a big skinhead… y'know, National Front thing...

MARK: Yeah, yeah, well I remember we played Blackburn town hall, through Alan Wise. It was quite like 'Where are we then?' It just got smashed up, the whole place. And I thought 'how dated this is' y'know.

This is a weird thing; my Grandad, when he got back from Dunkirk, he was assigned to Blackburn y'know: to watch the people.

GRAHAM: In what way?

MARK: Well, he was at Dunkirk. But he got honourably discharged because he killed these SS men. So they had to find summat for him to do. He was a Sergeant Major. So, he used to go to fuckin'

Blackburn. And they had to guard the factories in Blackburn. Coz there was sabotage: the Black Shirts. It was the Black Shirts! They wanted to be, alone with Rochdale, they wanted to be the puppet government of the Nazis, see?

I mean in Blackburn, in the Second World War… 60% of the cloth in the world came from fuckin' Britain. And half of that was from Blackburn, so they had more power than anybody really. Nobody would have any clothes!

▲ ▲ ▲

7

HOTEL FREUD

MARK: Where you staying?

GRAHAM: Just the *Ibis* on Princes Street. It's weird, there's no reception any more. There's just a young man and woman with a laptop, sitting on bar stools, and that's it. And they've all got red T-shirts that say 'Welcome Home'. Then in the rooms, there's no phones, so if you want to get an iron or whatever, you've got to text them using your own phone.

MARK: It's a fuckin' joke man. I was in this writing trial about a year ago. And this publisher fuckin' put me up in that Clement Freud's house in Maida Vale.

GRAHAM: Right. What, as a punishment?

(Laughter)

MARK: I had to stay over night. I had a separate block, y'know what I mean? To do this fuckin' stupid creative writer's trial.

GRAHAM: Why Clement Freud's house?

MARK: Y'know, where the psychiatrist lived.

GRAHAM: Oh right, *Sigmund* Freud.

MARK: Yeah. It's where he lived in Maida Vale. It's been a hotel for years. I forgot to remember. But it's been like a B&B in fuckin' Maida Vale. It's just near my publisher – ex-publisher. So I was determined... Coz I stayed in this separate house. So I had to be y'know, getting in there ten o'clock the night before the trial, 'be up in the morning' y'know, read all the stuff... And the fuckin'... I get in this room and it must have been that part of the house that was his surgery, y'know what I mean?

GRAHAM: Oh really? Oh wow.

MARK: So I've got that side of the hotel to myself, y'know what I mean? So I walk in, it's just a goldmine going in the place. You've got Freudian problems by the time you get in the room!

(Laughter)

MARK: You walk up these fuckin' steps, then there's just more stairs. It's like *Psycho* or something. Then you go past this room. This room is just a table – a low table with about six chairs around it. And it looks like six people have just left the room. It's really spooky.

And you go up another fuckin' floor, and there's this massive big fuckin' bath! Biggest bath you've ever seen. I'd drove all the way up from Manchester, on speed of course! I don't wanna go to this trial, you know what I mean. I'm fuckin'... I'm fucked! And it's like a hundred and ninety quid a night this fuckin' hotel.

So I walk up another bleedin' flight, and I finally get into this room. And this room has like a fuckin' brass bed. A brass bed with knobs on it. And loads of like... Y'know, like somebody's taking the piss, like having psychiatry things y'know.

I could just about fit on this double bed. And it's all gold tassels. It's got like a hundred cushions on it, what women'd have, you know, to talk about their sexuality. But yeah y'know, it's alright, I can deal with this. But then, the phone starts. They've got like a little porta-phone. It just started ringing the minute I got in. And I couldn't work out how to answer it, and it went on like this. Like it was a Freud show. It went on like that for the next twelve hours. It kept ringing! I threw it against the wall! I went downstairs and put it in that shower thing!

(Laughter)

MARK: You know what the shower was like? You know where people shrink and the shower looks like... That's what it was, was like that.

Anyway I don't know why I'm telling you that. Ah! That's what it was: I had to go down to the front desk, which was locked certain times of day, in another building. And they said it's standard in London now, y'know. And it is. The posher the hotel… I mean, it's like yer don't wanna say it, but what if you have a fire? How do you ring reception?

GRAHAM: Exactly.

MARK: Say you're being murdered in your room, how d'yer ring down?

GRAHAM: So many of these things are disguised as being something else, when really it's just to save them money.

MARK: But there's free wi-fi yeah? Free wi-fi! Then they say they want a hundred and fifty quid deposit to open the phone line. That's the new one.

GRAHAM: A hundred and fifty quid for what?

MARK: In posh hotels. The Hilton and all that. So they can open… So they can do what they used to do anyway, y'know. *That's* a luxury hotel. You just pick up fuckin'… their line, and ring all your enemies and go "fuck off"!

(Laughter)

MARK: Most of the posts have been usurped. No, it's wrong, it's horrible – especially if you're trying to get somebody. Say I tried to ring you up y'know. They'd never tell you if you were in the room or not. So you end up with foreign journalists. They end up hanging around the hotel, hoping that someone comes out who looks Norwegian. It's fuckin' stupid y'know.

(Laughter)

▲ ▲ ▲

8

GANGSTER FILMS, TELEVISION & COINCIDENCE

MARK: What I've always liked, y'know… I like a few old films. Film is like how… the good ones, the old ones. They're not that long y'know. Like *White Heat* with James Cagney it's about one hour ten. You wouldn't think it. You watch it, it's just like fuckin' hell! Bam!! I was watching that one with what's he called? Brad Pitt: *Public Enemies* or something.

GRAHAM: I've not seen that. It's the thing about Capone is it?

MARK: No, it's where they're all in suits and it's happy hour. It's just about Dillinger an' that. It was on the other night. Can't have been out four years y'know. It's about three hours long. It wouldn't end. And you couldn't hear what they were sayin' y'know.

GRAHAM: There's a real vogue now for…

MARK: They mumble, they're all mumbling, to make it 'realistic'.

GRAHAM: Yeah. It's that thing… something can seem realistic, but that doesn't necessarily mean it's interesting.

MARK: It's not.

GRAHAM: A lot of the best film is really stylized y'know. I don't think it has to be film's job to present the real world.

MARK: I know. Well it's not the real world is it. It's fuckin'… people who've been to film school – the art school. It's like music's the same. I mean come on! Every girl rapper has been to fuckin'… a London art class, y'know. It is the whole thing, y'know. Talent shows…

GRAHAM: It's like going back to the notion of Tin Pan Alley isn't it really. All this sort of *X-Factor* stuff is just encouraging people to think 'oh you just learn a bunch of songs that are already famous, work on your chops and that's good enough.'

MARK: It's like the old Guinness advert isn't it y'know. *(posh voice)* "The rain in Spain". Give her a fuckin' can of Heineken. And she goes *(cockney drawl)* "The raaain in Spain…". A fuckin' 60s joke isn't it: the false cockney accent and all that. I mean it *is* Tommy Steele. It's a Damon Albarn world isn't it really. What he wanted. Hey that could make a good episode!

GRAHAM: Damon Albarn World?

MARK: Damon Albarn World!

(Laughter)

MARK: D'yer remember, I told you his favourite musical is *Oh What a Lovely War*?

GRAHAM: Oh yeah.

MARK: What about that *Who Do You Think You Are?* Have you ever watched that?

GRAHAM: No. Well, I saw some of the Paxman one, a couple of bits.

MARK: So many of them celebrities turn out to have really crooked pasts. Have you ever noticed? I mean if I was them, I'd say 'Stop now!' wouldn't you?

GRAHAM: What, before you find out too much?

MARK: Yeah. It's a boring programme. It's like… it's what I've always thought, because I can read faces, y'know what I mean. I am pretty shrewd at that. And I've always thought certain people they just look bad. Like Nigel Lawson I always thought. I mean like Nigella Lawson.

(Laughter)

MARK: It's unwatchable, that programme. But it could be useful, about three minutes of it in something. It is very *Twilight Zoney*. Don't go into your past y'know. That is the inherent message.

GRAHAM: It's that idea… having more information about the past can change how you behave in the present. It's like someone starting to behave with airs and graces because they find out they're distantly related to some Duke.

MARK: I have a weird thing, which is very... If I think of anybody and I switch the TV on, and their face comes on. Happens all the time.

GRAHAM: Really?

MARK: Happens all the time... Like for instance, when we were going to Ireland right, as we were taking off I was fuckin' seriously crashing to be honest. And I knew I was gonna y'know… it's like you know you're going to have this revelation…

The flight from fuckin' Manchester to Ireland is great. It's like fuckin' half an hour. And who walks up the fuckin' aisle but *Bez*. Anyway, he's in a white jumper Bez, and all his hair's grey. And I wanted to ask him if he had any fuckin' drugs on him. But it wasn't appropriate. And I'd just been thinking "If Bez was here…"

(Laughter)

MARK: Coz I'm going to Ireland and I know I'm not gonna get anything for the next three days. Not that I'm a fuckin' junkie or anything. But then you think like that don't yer, coz it's half fuckin' six in the morning and you're like urrrgh.

But then Bez walks up which was really good y'know what I mean. And you wanna fuckin' say "Bez! What yer got?" But then it's "Everybody fasten yer seat belts" y'know. It's one of those things you can't do. Coz you know you're gonna get thrown off don't yer, you know what I mean? I'm sweaty. "Bez!!" Sat with a load of big, fat Irish businessmen. You know it's not gonna go down.

So anyway, so I get home, on the couch for a week, ill *(laughs)*. I'm just thinking about that incident. I switch *Granada Reports* on. *Bez* comes up in his white pullover and he wants to introduce pigeons or something … No, he wants to introduce bees to fuckin' Manchester.

GRAHAM: What?

MARK: No, it's not really convincing is it?

(Laughter)

GRAHAM: It's weird though isn't it? People tend to think coincidences are these rare things, but coincidences are far more common than that. There's a really obvious pattern to stuff some times.

MARK: Oh aye.

GRAHAM: About a year ago, I was shifting some crap in the garden and I had a Throbbing Gristle album playing. An electronic thing and I was thinking 'fucking hell, this really reminds me of Tangerine Dream'. And it was a track I'd been listening to for years and years. But you know when you suddenly hear something in a slightly different way? And I thought 'I used to have a couple of early Tangerine Dream albums years ago. I should try and get them again.'

And then my mobile buzzed in my pocket. And it was my sister Susan's husband: Simon. It was a text saying "I'm getting rid of a load of records. I've got a few Tangerine Dream albums, would you want them?" What a coincidence y'know.

MARK: Really?

GRAHAM: And then, about a week later I was in London with Malcolm. And we were in a bar, and I was telling him the story. "I was in the garden, thinking about Tangerine Dream and my brother-in-law texted me saying do you want these Tangerine Dream albums". Malcolm goes "Oh that's weird."

Then my phone goes again in my pocket and it's Simon saying "Just sent you those Tangerine Dream albums in the post". So it was like, as soon as I mentioned it again, it came up. So yeah... I don't read anything into it. But when this stuff happens you think well that's...

MARK: Yeah, yeah. Have you ever had that where you think of people, and they turn up on the fuckin' front door, y'know? Freaks me out. It's happened to me once or twice.

GRAHAM: But do you get that thing as well, where you'll be walking around town or wherever and you'll see someone and you'll think oh that's y'know, Bob or whoever? But it's not. But then ten minutes later you actually see the person that you thought it was.

MARK: No I've never had that one! That's interesting isn't it?

GRAHAM: I have that one quite a bit.

MARK: Oh that's weird isn't it. That is a weird one isn't it!

GRAHAM: It's like... I dunno... without wanting to sound too wholemeal it's like their energy was, was...

MARK: ...in the vicinity. So what do you do when you see the real one?

GRAHAM: I always say "Oh I thought I saw you."

MARK: You're not prepared?

GRAHAM: I don't know.

MARK: I always get this thing, where I get this person in my mind. Then I sort of force it out... force it out. A lot of the time it's a woman and I'm just not interested. So a lot of time it's a negative… and I force it out and it's just… I just sort of deal with it very well.

Then erm, I'll walk 'round the corner and there'll be that person. Y'know, they'll just go "it's all in your fuckin' head". You know what I mean? Know what I'm saying? If you haven't got any power, you haven't got any fuckin'... So shut up about it y'know. And you'll just be going along, very happy, very relaxed and they'll fuckin' come out of nowhere. It's like a delayed sort of... But you've got one that goes first!

GRAHAM: Yeah.

MARK: You've got a warning thing haven't you?

GRAHAM: Yeah. I had this idea a little while ago. It's quite a Philip K. Dick idea in a way. I was going around this supermarket and I was quite stoned, and I was having that thing where I was thinking 'Is that such and such a person?' No, it's just that they had that sort of look. Y'know as you get older, people tend to fall into types more readily.

MARK: Right, right.

GRAHAM: And the idea is about this man who starts seeing people as types. He sees less and less variation in people, until in the end he can only see one kind of man and one kind of woman.

MARK: Well it's the truth!

(Laughter)

MARK: I've been all over the world. It's the truth! It's the truth! I've always thought there's only ten or eleven. There's only twelve people in the world. There's only twelve people.

GRAHAM: Do you think they're the original tribes?

MARK: No, no, no.

GRAHAM: No? What is it then?

MARK: There's only six. I've noticed. I know and I've been... There's only one kind of Russian now. There used to be loads of types of Russians. There's only a couple of types of Germans now. When I first went to Germany, there were a lot of types of Germans, y'know what I'm sayin'?

I mean come on, you're from Lancashire. There were a lot of different types of fuckin' Lancastrians, of our age. I mean come on, y'know all them lunatics, y'know. I mean do you remember all them loonies in fuckin' Blackburn?

GRAHAM: Oh yeah, real rough, rough lads.

MARK: Chucking pint pots – but also very clever. They're all... It's a form of communism.

GRAHAM: But is it TV saying to people you must aspire to a certain lifestyle?

MARK: It softens up their brains a bit.

GRAHAM: Well, there's that, but also... it's like you're taught what you should aspire to. We're fed all these images from *Big Brother* or whatever.

MARK: They haven't got a filter system have they? What I'm saying is they haven't got a filter system. Like I have, or you have.

GRAHAM: No, but then you're, for want of a better word, sophisticated aren't you? Y'know, you're a thinker. A lot of people aren't.

MARK: Oh course not. Like I understand where they're at. They've got jobs to do and all that: kids and all. But y'know, I can see their shoes. It doesn't take much to drag 'em out of their fuckin' depths, but it's just hard work in my personal experience.

▲ ▲ ▲

9

DREAM OF 400 PROPAGANDA FILMS

MARK: I had this dream, where there was 400 films made by the Americans, during the Second World War: propaganda films that featured three brothers. This is what I actually thought, in me head y'know, was reality.

I was telling these African people at around ten o'clock at night, how these films used to come out during the Second World War, where you'd have Laurel and Hardy. You know 'em! I'm talking to you in the same way! Where Laurel and Hardy and maybe Stan Laurel's brother, or Oliver's brother would join 'em. And the three of them would volunteer for the army to fight the Japanese.

I'm going to this old African woman:

"You remember them don't yer?"

(v. high pitched) "That kind of film doesn't exist!"

Then there'd be *The Three O'Mulligans Go To War*. And there'd be another one called… for the Germany audience it'd be *The Three Fritzheimers Go To War* – you remember 'em!

"There's no way you can get 'em!" I said to these Africans.

But it had all these film series, y'know like you'd see on *Breaking Bad* and all that. I believed myself that they existed. You know, like Bob Hope and his two brothers join the army. Like *Saving Private Ryan* but 30s.

▲ ▲ ▲

10

RECORD COMPANIES & 'WORKING FROM HOME'

GRAHAM: I got that Can *Lost Tapes.*

MARK: Oh right, yeah?

GRAHAM: Have you heard it?

MARK: Yeah, yeah. What the big fuckin'…?

GRAHAM: The box set, yeah.

MARK: Yeah, it's hard work isn't it?

GRAHAM: There's too much of it really. But…

MARK: There's a good Malcolm Mooney one. What is it like…? 'I Am Me' or something? What is it? The Malcolm Mooney one: it's like fuckin'… he had to stop. I like that. No I think it should have been lost that.

(Laughter)

GRAHAM: What, you think it should have never been discovered? There must be hours of it still. You can't digest it all at once, but there's some great things on there.

MARK: Oh definitely, definitely. I forgot about that. I was gonna bring you some crap down. Those country and western ones y'know, the ones they sell on the fuckin' shopping channels.

GRAHAM: Like trucker's songs and stuff?

MARK: Yeah, yeah. I give most of them away, to some grateful people. But erm... I'm trying to compile a live LP and it's just... I don't really wanna do it. It's like it's a weird situation.

GRAHAM: Live Fall stuff?

MARK: Yeah, yeah, from the last fuckin' years. Like fuckin' 2008 to now.

GRAHAM: Well if you want any sleeve notes doing...

MARK: Yeah, you do 'em. Yeah. Like a fool I gave away... I had that fuckin' Brighton one that you were at, that you said about. I gave it to the fuckin'... the bleedin' rat catcher.

(Laughter)

GRAHAM: What is it, a desk recording?

MARK: Yeah, yeah, yeah.

GRAHAM: Is that the only copy? Has that gone?

MARK: No, no. But I mean... where do you start, y'know? I can't be objective. Fact is, Cherry Red have compiled their own y'see – of *their* favourites. And it can't go out. It's just the worse thing you've ever heard in your bleedin' life, y'know.

GRAHAM: Poor recordings or...?

MARK: No, it's stuff I've give 'em and stuff they've got y'know.

GRAHAM: But you don't think it's good enough?

MARK: No, half of it can go out y'know. It's just the fans who work in the record company. Y'know what I mean? It does need to be done. But how can I sit down and listen to it?

GRAHAM: It is very hard to be objective about your own stuff.

MARK: That's what I'm sayin' y'know. I know it's not a big deal. But y'know, typical... They don't think you're on the ball y'see. I did the EP straight away. And it only turns out this week... they're so fuckin' computerized. They all work at home nowadays. So you think *you've* got fuckin' problems, y'know what I mean?

It's a fuckin' EP man! You can't just ring the fuckin' office. Coz y'know, the guy you're dealing with, he only works at this record company two days a week. He works with Universal one day a week. And he's freelancing – he won't say where – the other day of the week. The boss is on fuckin' holiday! The fuckin' one who does the fuckin' artwork, she only works Tuesday and Wednesday, y'know. It's like if they had an *office* y'know, then I could say...

And I have to post all the artwork off and all the track listings, and I have to talk to the guys. But it's like if they just had an office, the five of them sat together, from ten 'til five... I mean what's the matter? But they all think they're all *'working from home'*. They're all *'working from home'*. Y'know, I mean it's the biggest con, I think. *You're* a writer, that's different. It is the biggest con. They're all *'working from home'*. Well, you're not working from home! Y'know?

It's only a 6-track EP. But y'know at the end of the day... it always happens! You leave it to them, you send 'em the emails – I don't deal with 'em. I always say "use the phone". They never use the fuckin' telephone. So they always have to come to me through email. Y'know, so it's like... If they all just fuckin' got together, four hours a fuckin' day, like Americans do. Americans, they get together, even the shittiest... They go in at six in the morning, they knock off at two.

It's fuckin'... it's Cherry Red, y'know what I mean? We just give 'em the only top 40 LP they've ever had, y'know in the last twenty years. And still they're trying to get a live LP and all this, you know what I mean, it's like... You wonder why British industry... You just get fed up in the end. But no, do some sleeve notes, that'll be good. That'll confuse 'em! That'll confuse 'em! I'll send you a track listing tomorrow. I'll send you a load of track names and say... make it up.

GRAHAM: I can make things up.

(Laughter)

MARK: If you can imagine it, I've got things like 'Hamburg Wedding'. No God bless 'em, the Cherry Red one's are alright: 'Croydon 1984' y'know. *(laughs)* 'Psychick Dancehall'... It sounds like it's recorded in your fuckin' toilet.

GRAHAM: Is this something you want to bring out this year?

MARK: Yeah.

GRAHAM: For the Christmas market?

(Laughter)

MARK: I don't think so!

GRAHAM: Do you just say "right, this is the track list, this is the order of the tracks"? Do they ever try and say "no, we want..."

MARK: No, not at all.

GRAHAM: Is that in the contract?

MARK: Well it's better for them isn't it? Then they can blame you.

▲ ▲ ▲

11

FLACKA, SPICE, STRYCHNINE, ACID, AZTEC TEA, ECSTASY, SPEED, KETAMINE & WHISKY

GRAHAM: I was looking online, about this drug called Flacka. Have you heard about that?

MARK: No.

GRAHAM: It's a legal high. It's in two or three states in America. A bit like Spice. A bunch of herbs and they spray it with this stuff. So it can be anything. It just turns people into psychopaths. There's this footage – you'd think you were watching a zombie movie.

There's people with blood 'round their mouths, just staggering around. Some guy in a car park – CCTV footage – he just runs across this car park, dives through the back window of a stationary car. Actually smashes his way through. He comes out, starts biting his arm.

MARK: Flacka?

GRAHAM: Yeah. There's people biting off their own skin. The high must have to be pretty good to validate that!

MARK: So you just smoke it like Spice, in a single skin?

GRAHAM: Yeah you just smoke it in pipes and stuff.

MARK: Did you ever have any of that Spice?

GRAHAM: No.

MARK: This fuckin' twat I know, he put some in a joint: Spice. Without tellin' us. Fuckin' hell, it made you fuckin' ill.

GRAHAM: So what did it make you feel like?

MARK: It was like a bad erm… I had about two pints, and a couple of tugs on this joint. I was really kickin' up. It was this fuckin' Spice. Then I felt dead sick. I felt dead sick for about a day, y'know. Spitting up the taste of cannabis. I thought 'this is a first in my mind'. It was horrible. It's like you see on telly, and you laugh, see 'em in Piccadilly Gardens. And you think nobody's that out of it. It was like that. I thought it'd be just like bad pot y'know.

GRAHAM: Yeah, I'd assumed that, but that it made you feel sick.

MARK: I can't see the point of making it horrible as well, y'know. I can't see any reason for that. What they'd sprayed on it is summat daft. Just to make it… Like they used to put cyanide in acid. Rat poison.

GRAHAM: Strychnine.

MARK: Yeah, strychnine. Used to put it in acid: if the acid was too good. This is drug-dealers for you. In the 70s, when the acid got too pure, people'd put strychnine in it. So they'd pay more for it. You always used to know when the strychnine was in it. Because you'd feel depressed while you were tripping. Obviously, because you were being poisoned, y'know.

GRAHAM: I'm not sure I could take hallucinogens again now. It's probably about ten years since last time I took some mushrooms.

MARK: Is it?

GRAHAM: How long since you did a trip? I reckon it's about ten years for me.

MARK: Me too. We should get some! The last good stuff I had was in that place near Matt and Phred's. The Aztec Tea. That was fuckin' great. This Aztec Tea, it's just like a red leaf. Mad Jewish feller, he lives on his own. This Jewish man-lad he got me this Aztec Tea. It's Aztec stuff. What a trip it was. Like real old acid: like Peyote.

GRAHAM: So what do you do, do you smoke it or…?

MARK: It's like… It was stale, so I thought it wouldn't be any good. But you'd eat like a couple of crumbs of it. It was like… you know like when mushrooms were really good? When you first had them and you went "Wow!" It's like that. But it was just a few flakes, y'know.

GRAHAM: Aztec tea. There's always more. With pills, I suspect a lot of it is just variations on E. With ecstasy it's the day after that I don't like. It's the residual feeling of anxiety.

MARK: Fuckin' hell… You're tellin' me.

GRAHAM: I've only done it a handful times. It's not really the drug for me.

MARK: I tell yer what, you notice the casualties of ecstasy quicker than anything else. I'm seein' 'em now. You know when you go to these Haçienda evenings that Phil goes to. There's people there, they're like 55 – younger than me. And they dance like this *(jerks arms)*. From 20 years of doing E y'know. And you can see, it's more prevailing than a whisky drinker. It's like they're still having the process where they come down the next day. Like they do off speed, y'know. They're trying to dance and they…

GRAHAM: I think a lot of people who've done loads of E are quite depressed as well.

MARK: Very much.

GRAHAM: It's like it gives you all your joy in one burst. And then there's none left, y'know.

MARK: That was what the bad amphetamines were like, yeah. What ecstasy does to your brain is like that. It just squeezes all the juices out. And this is what makes me laugh about them false drugs y'see. Cocaine stays in your system.

What they do, they squeeze all the orange out. So you're *gonna* get depressed. It's a force: you've paid for that. You've had it, and you've got to pay for it like a bank loan. It's how they design the drug. No, you've got to pay for it y'know. Which is why 'depressed' won't be in it, y'know.

GRAHAM: A lot of people who I know, who were big ravers, they're all fucking low now...

MARK: Oh they were painfully happy weren't they? I mean I could have killed somebody me.

GRAHAM: *(laughs)* What for being that happy?

MARK: No, being on E, I wanted to kill people! I didn't love anybody. But you could see they were just washing it out of their brain. It was quite hurtful for me. There's a night on the E. They never said "Oh you might die, you might have a brain seizure". The reason you have a brain seizure is the brain's going 'this is not what the brain's used for'. It's not used for tasting chocolate every ten seconds y'know. It's used to think.

At least with say, speed, you get so you feel shit, but your body's replacing itself. And it's kicked a lot of parts of your brain that wouldn't be kicked off. Ecstasy doesn't do that. It just gives you all the physical and the urm... y'know. Coz the people who were doing E, were the people who shouldn't have done E. If you're fit, it's the worst thing you could do is E.

GRAHAM: I suppose I was always quite suspicious of ecstasy, because it's that thing of commonality y'know. "Come on! Love everybody!" And y'know, that's not true. I *don't* love everybody, because there's a lot of fucking dicks in the world. So I don't need a drug that convinces me that everybody's brilliant.

MARK: Because they're not!

(Laughter)

GRAHAM: No.

MARK: That was the freakiest thing. I remember going to the Haçienda one night, and I saw this gang of builders from 'round here. I didn't like 'em at all. They were like enemies of *my* mate: these builders, who were coke-takers. But they were all on fuckin'… 'M People'. And they came over, and they were dead nice. And it was more frightening than when they used to threaten me and throw me off ladders and everything!

I was more frightened when they came over and they said they loved me. I was fuckin' shitting it!

"Oh we don't mean anything against you and JR, or anybody! Or Mad Graham or anybody! We love you Mark! We always have! We didn't mean it when we said yer singing's shit!" And all this. I was like "Just stay there! Don't come near me!"

GRAHAM: It's like the kiss of death from the Mafia isn't it?

MARK: I had a glass of whisky in me hand. And I was like anointing them! Talk about *them* being nuts. I was fuckin' as well. I had a whisky and I'm going "anoint!" y'know. "Get away from me!" Coz that's why I started drinking whisky, to get off the fuckin' E and the Ketamine. It really worked.

▲ ▲ ▲

'Once talking was my favourite while
But now I know a conversation's end
Before it's done'

'Living Too Late' – Mark E. Smith

LAST ORDERS

Saturday November 12th 2017

I travel up from Brighton to Manchester. The following day I'm due to direct the recording of two Count Arthur Strong Christmas Specials for Radio 4 at the Lowry Theatre in Salford. Whilst on the train I've been going through the scripts, adding new gags and making notes. I've worked diligently, but I've also been feeling distracted.

I check into the hotel, take a shower then phone for a cab to drive me out to Prestwich. Although I haven't seen Mark since back in January, when The Fall played in Brighton, we've talked a few times on the phone since he got his diagnosis. He has remained resolutely realistic about the ongoing situation.

Despite the diagnosis, The Fall have had a pretty busy year. Their fierce and abrasive new album *New Facts Emerge* was released at the end of July, with the group playing gigs in support of it. Whilst there have been some cancellations due to the vagaries of Mark's health, the gigs they have played have been a testament to his force of will. Just over a week ago The Fall appeared at the Queen Margaret Union Hall in Glasgow.

Online footage of the gig shows the group powering into 'Wolf Kidult Man' with Mark coming on stage down a ramp in a wheelchair to an enormous cheer. He then proceeds to give a performance of near feral commitment.

Yet, away from his responsibilities with the group, Mark has generally been lying low and avoiding seeing people. I know he's been having a tough time recovering from the chemotherapy and I thought it unlikely he'd be in the mood for visitors. But I couldn't come up to Manchester without at least asking.

Rather than bothering him directly, I'd sent a Facebook message to his girlfriend Pam. I'd asked if she thought Mark might feel up to a brief visit. She replied the next day, saying he'd love to see me.

The taxi pulls up outside Pam's house in Prestwich. As I approach the front door I'm nervous. I wish I wasn't. But I am.

It's not the nervousness I felt just over a decade ago, as I waited for Mark to arrive at the BBC building on Oxford Road. I'm not saying back then I was an acolyte praying that whatever I had to say would be worthy of his master's ears. However, I'd be lying if I didn't admit there was at least a hint of that.

Since then, we've talked so much and *about* so much that I've become loose-lipped in Mark's presence. Not as loose-lipped as Mark obviously. But then few are. Right now, the nervousness I feel is because I'm about to visit a friend who is dying. And it seems unlikely that whatever I have to say will be worthy of the situation.

Pam opens the door. We've never met before and these are obviously far from ideal circumstances for a first meeting. Nevertheless she greets me kindly. As I'm taking off my coat a familiar voice calls out from the living room, "A'right Graham?"

I walk through to see Mark sitting on the sofa. Dressed in black slacks and a grey shirt, he looks small and scrawny. He's also sporting a full beard. Something I never thought I'd see.

He asks if I want a drink but I tell him I've given up alcohol as it was screwing up my digestion.

"Join the club," he says with a snort. "I can't either. I've got a red raw mouth from the chemo."

Mark talks a little about his illness. Although his tales of being in hospital display his own slanted take on reality and are undoubtedly adulterated by the unpredictable balm of morphine. When he tells me how his hospital bed had "dropped away into a laundry chute" I'm unsure if he's speaking literally, metaphorically or hallucinogenically.

He's been prescribed liquid morphine whilst recuperating from the effects of chemo. He shows me a box containing a huge, brown glass bottle of morphine about the size of a whisky bottle. I admire the stark design of the box.

"I wanted to make a cover out of it," says Mark. "Stick some bananas around it."

"Painkillers don't work on me obviously," he says. "But morphine? Nature's built it. The pain goes. It's a fuckin' wonder drug. What it does make you do is see things very clearly. Through a morphine haze like they describe. But it's very cold and smoky."

Despite the pain, despite the exhaustion, despite the morphine, Mark will be lucid and focussed for the entire evening. We sit and talk about the stuff we always talk about: mutual friends, music, the music industry, drugs, books, films.

I give him a copy of Philip K. Dick's *Dr. Bloodmoney* as I had recalled him saying it was one of just a few of the author's novels he hadn't read. Mark says he's been watching lots of DVDs, including P.T. Anderson's *There Will Be Blood* and the grubby pleasures of Jim Hosking's *The Greasy Strangler*, as well as re-watching his personal favourites: Billy Wilder's *Ace in the Hole*, Roman Polanski's *Macbeth* and Lindsay Anderson's *Britannia Hospital.*

As always, the best part of the conversation is when Mark slips into telling anecdotes. Stories that take unexpected turns and go on wild divergences. Rants that could not possibly have come from anyone else's loose lips. And we laugh. A lot. After one anecdote, Mark clears his throat and smiles.

"Sorry, I'm a bit cheerful today Graham," he says, before adding. "I've had a rough two days".

"What happens when you finish the chemo?" I ask. He screws up his face.

"Either this'll kill it off, or just keep it dormant. Unless it's fuckin' out of control – then I die I suppose".

In a week's time, The Fall are due to fly to Portugal to play a gig at a club in Porto. He confidently tells me he's still planning to do this. I feel a doubt I don't express. Sitting on the sofa, winnowed by the cancer, he looks so infirm. I think it's unlikely he'll be well enough to undertake the journey, never mind play the gig. There's no point in saying this of course. Even now, having been brought to a savage standstill by the disease, he still exudes determination.

Mark mentions that the MTV Europe Awards are being televised tonight. I'm surprised by how keen he is to watch them. Although to be honest, whenever something comes on that he doesn't like – which is frequently – Mark switches to another channel for a minute or so, thereby intercutting the MTV awards with bursts of local news reports, commercials and fragments of some romantic drama series.

It would be easy for me to start thinking he's doing a real time Burroughsian cut-up. But in truth it's just another example of how Mark approaches life: rearranging and refashioning as he goes.

On screen, Stormzy is required to do some presenting. The rapper lapses into monosyllabic utterances.

"He's a laugh a minute that feller isn't he," says Mark. "Full o' quips."

During the award for Best Alternative Act, the banal pap of the aptly named Clean Bandit pumps from the TV. Mark hums along sarcastically. For something that's being labelled Alternative it sounds remarkably like Eurovision.

"This is what it's like in America," says Mark. "American alternative is like cabaret music. It's like Carole King."

A clip comes up of Lorde singing 'Green Light'. Mark growls with glee. It turns out he's recently seen the episode of *South Park* which features a piss-take of the singer.

"I thought she was just the invention of *South Park*," he says with a dry cackle.

He shows me a stylish brown and silver cassette recorder he's bought in order to record audio from the TV. He plays me a bit of Glen Campbell he recorded earlier in the week. I check the time on my phone. I suddenly realise we've been talking for over three hours.

"I should probably be going. I've got an early start in the morning." I haven't really. But it feels more respectful to say this rather than 'I don't want to tire you out.'

Before I go, Mark wants to play me something. We sit and listen to the first side of Marty Robbins's 1959 country and western album *Gunfighter Ballads & Trail Songs*. I've never heard it before. It contains slow, mournful country tunes such as 'Big Iron' and 'Billy the Kid'. Robbins's smooth, reverb drenched voice bounces around the white suburban walls.

"It's a fuckin' weird LP this," says Mark. "It's all about the baddie's side."

Now it really is time to go. Pam phones for a cab. It arrives frustratingly quickly. I button up my coat. I lean over and hug Mark's thin frame.

"Marvellous to see you Graham," he says, smiling broadly.

"And you mate," I say. "I'll see you soon."

But I know I won't.

LIST OF ILLUSTRATIONS

THANKS & ACKNOWLEDGEMENTS

Elena Poulou – For your friendship, support and care, for your inspirational music and art, and for all your years of devotion to both Mark and The Fall. Thank you for your beautiful essay and photographs, and for believing in the project in the first place.

Malcolm Boyle – For your friendship, your inspired notes, and for guiding me back to The Fall when I fell out of love in the mid 80s.

Imogen Christie – For your positive comments on the first draft of the script and your subsequent insights on the essays.

Stephen Thrower – For your encouragement and excellent notes.

Phil Fennings & James Fennings – For being there for Mark when it mattered.

Misha Begley – For knowing a good thing when you heard it and for making me very proud indeed.

Pete Cowie – For listening to me going on about The Fall for most of our lives.

Thanks also go to John Blackett, Tobi Blackman, Christine Duff, Kirsty Elmer, Tanja Ganger, Daren Garrett, Peter Greenway, Graham Humphreys, Phil Jones, Keiron Melling, Jim Moir, Simon Ounsworth, Tim Presley, Dave Spurr, Deborah Turnbull, Johnny Vegas, Alan Wise and all the members of The Fall between 1976 and 2018.

'Ours is not to look back
Ours is to continue the craic'

'Fantastic Life' – Mark E. Smith

STRANGE ATTRACTOR PRESS
2021